'Why did you leave and why are you back?' Ben demanded.

Abbie sucked in her breath, touched a tiny gold pin on the shoulder of her coat. 'I'm sorry, Ben. I wanted to spare you.'

'Spare me?' He shook his head in disbelief. 'We were about to promise for better or for worse, in sickness and in health—'

'I'm not saying I'd do the same thing all over again. But I can't change the past. At the time, leaving seemed absolutely right.'

'For whom?' Anger crackled in his words, but then his expression turned tender. 'I'm sorry about what you've been through,' he said, his voice gruff. 'But you're okay?'

'I'm okay.' She smiled, that same soft smile that could light up a room, that could turn his insides to mush. 'And I've finally come home.'

Dear Reader,

Welcome to Silhouette Special Edition, to a world full of life, love and family.

Allison Leigh effortlessly picks up the baton in THE STOCKWELLS family books with *Her Unforgettable Fiancé*, where proximity provokes passion in a couple who should have married years ago. And there's another couple who should have become a couple a long time ago, but when they do get together it's really special—look for *At the Heart's Command* by Patricia McLinn, which has another linked book coming next month, too.

Marie Ferrarella returns once more with a touching book about a father who's given up everything to keep his three daughters safe, *Father Most Wanted*, and if you're a fan of Marie's you'll be delighted to know that she has a new book next month also. There's another dad in Suzanne Carey's *When Love Walks In*, but the twist is that he doesn't know he has a son.

Susan Mallery's *Wife in Disguise* is the last of her LONE STAR CANYON books where an accident makes Josie Scott rethink what's important to her—her sexy ex-husband. And finally our THAT'S MY BABY! title is a little different this month even though it still has a cute baby in it; do let us know what you think of *A Bundle of Miracles* from Amy Frazier.

Enjoy them all.

The Editors

A Bundle of Miracles

AMY FRAZIER

SILHOUETTE®

SPECIAL EDITION™

*First published in Great Britain 2002
Silhouette Books, Eton House, 18-24 Paradise Road,
Richmond, Surrey TW9 1SR*

© Amy Lanz 2000

ISBN 0 373 24354 5

23-0302

*Printed and bound in Spain
by Litografia Rosés S.A., Barcelona*

AMY FRAZIER

has loved to listen to, read and tell stories from the time she was a very young child. With the support of a loving family, she grew up believing she could accomplish anything she set her mind to. It was with this attitude that she tackled various careers as a teacher, librarian, freelance artist, professional storyteller, wife and mother. Above all else, the stories always beckoned. It is with a contented sigh that she settles into the romance field, where she can weave stories in which love conquers all.

Amy now lives with her husband, son and daughter in northwest Georgia, where the kudzu grows high as an elephant's eye. When not writing, she loves reading, music, painting, gardening, bird-watching and the Atlanta Braves.

Dedicated to the sisters of survival, and in loving memory of those who left the field too soon.

Chapter One

"Oh, no! Not this cottage!" Abbie Latham fingered the angel pin she always wore on her shoulder. "Murphy," she muttered to the little gilt talisman, "is this your idea of a practical joke?"

"I beg your pardon?" Serena Hopkins, Point Narrows Realtor, set her Volvo's emergency brake. She turned a look of confusion upon Abbie.

"I didn't realize," Abbie explained hastily, "when you said you had the perfect rental ready for immediate occupancy that it would be this property." A rush of bittersweet memory engulfed her as she stared at the tiny white Victorian dripping with gingerbread trim. How had she expected to anesthetize the past?

"You know the place?"

Know it? Abbie had dreamed of living here one

day. With Ben. The past linked with the future. Two forbiddens in her quest to live only in the present.

"I've always loved it," she murmured, drinking in the sight of the December-bare rosebushes tumbling over the picket fence in the early-afternoon sun. She and Ben had discussed trimming back those bushes, Ben insisting the thorns would be a menace to their children as they played in the yard. Now the rose canes flourished where there'd be no children. None of Ben and Abbie's making, anyway.

Abbie's hard-won emotional balance listed slightly. She took a deep breath to retrieve it.

"Well, then, you're in luck." Serena turned off the car's ignition, adjusted her designer scarf in the V of her immaculately tailored camel coat and moved into Realtor mode. "The people who inherited it want to use it as a summer vacation house. But they need a winter tenant. To help defray costs. To keep an eye on the place. It's furnished and it's available as soon as you can unpack." Serena paused as Abbie made no move to get out of the car. "Of course, the rent is exceptionally cheap because you'll have to vacate during the months of July and August."

Mesmerized, Abbie stared at the cottage, which stood out from its plain New England clapboard neighbors like a petit four on a plate of chowder crackers. "I have no problem with relocating for two months in the summer," she murmured, consciously controlling the urge to think that far ahead. At the moment, the future wasn't the issue. She needed strength to deal with the past now flooding her emotions.

Serena reached out a leather-gloved hand. "I'm

sensing you do have some kind of problem with this property.''

"No." Steeling her will, Abbie opened the car door and relished the rush of bracing seaside air. "It's just that I saw myself owning the place one day, not renting."

"You and a friend of mine." With an elegance of motion Abbie envied, Serena stepped out of the car. "He was beside himself when he found out the property wasn't going on the market after Lily Arrondise died."

"Perhaps the heirs will tire of being long-distance landlords." Abbie smiled at the memory of lovely, never-married Miss Arrondise dispensing homemade molasses cookies and lemonade to the neighborhood children. This cottage should carry on the loving tradition, should be someone's home, a testament to day-to-day living, not an occasional vacation retreat or a temporary rental. "I can only hope."

"If the heirs put it up for sale, you'll find yourself in a bidding war with Ben Chase. He's determined to have this house."

"*Who* wants the house?" Incredulity stole over Abbie.

"Ben Chase. The police chief." A soft expression swept Serena's perfectly proportioned features. "He wants this place with a passion, which is kind of ironic, considering the cottage is so frilly, and Ben is so—"

"I *know* Ben." Abbie cut Serena off before she could go into vivid details about Ben's masculine characteristics.

"Do you, now?" A shadow of interest crept into the Realtor's cool blue eyes.

"I grew up in Point Narrows," Abbie replied, reining her voice back to noncommittal even as her heart sang a quick hallelujah chorus at the memory of her intimate knowledge of one Ben Chase.

"Well, I only moved here three years ago. From Boston. To get out of the rat race." Serena spread her hands over her heart in a dramatic gesture. "From my first visit this town called to me. It's special. Solid. Genuine. A place to meet a real man, get married and raise a family."

Abbie knew the compulsion. "And have you done all this?"

"Well, I have…met a very real man, but nothing's come of it…*yet*." Serena suddenly seemed appalled at her personal digression. "What am I thinking of? You want to see the house." She fumbled for keys in her coat pocket, her clumsiness in marked contrast to her physical perfection.

Abbie stared hard at Serena Hopkins and instantly saw a woman smitten with Ben Chase. She didn't blame her. Women naturally gravitated to Ben's strength of character and rugged good looks. Once, Ben had had eyes only for Abbie. He'd been hers. Unquestionably. Then she'd given him up.

It followed that she'd given up the right to the niggling stab of jealousy she now felt. Sure, she'd given up that right, but she couldn't quite control the pang's existence.

This sudden, unexpected possessiveness arose in marked opposition to her well-thought-out decision to return to Point Narrows, to explain to Ben—calmly, rationally—why she'd left him eight years ago. As soon as she could make him understand her departure, perhaps they could be friends. If not—she couldn't control the reactions of others—she'd still settle in the only place she'd ever considered home, would still concentrate on living day-to-day in a state of emotional balance, of hope laced with reality.

Her original goal remained intact, but her composure had just now taken a hit, making her search for closure a little tougher.

Ben Chase nearly ran his cruiser off the road.

It was his own fault.

From the moment this morning when Serena had told him over coffee at the Wayside Café that she was showing the cottage as a rental to an Abbie Latham newly arrived from Texas, he'd vowed to stay off the Leeward Road.

The local lobstermen called this kind of brilliant winter day a weather-breeder, a harbinger of trouble ahead. In Ben and Abbie's case, the brewing storm formed along unresolved fronts of emotional conflict. Meteorology had nothing to do with it. A sensible man, he'd promised himself he'd avoid Lily Arrondise's cottage so that hurt pride and suppressed anger would have no chance to fog and foul one beautiful day.

But as the appointment time drew near, he found himself in his cruiser, flying in the face of good sense, heading down the Leeward Road, toward Abbie and an explanation of her disappearance eight years ago.

Hell, he'd convinced himself he might as well get the confrontation over sooner than later. He needed her to explain, not to salve any hurt. No, he didn't hurt. He'd long ago gotten over her. He needed her to say her piece face-to-face, to clarify her decision and then to stand up to the consequences of her actions.

Call him a truth-and-consequences kind of guy.

Right now he simply wanted the truth.

Way back eight years ago her cryptic Dear John note—some bull about finding herself—had never satisfied him. He'd suspected she'd been pregnant. Pregnant with his child. Especially since her parents, Grant and Celeste Latham, had pulled up stakes, sold their house and left town with Abbie. Ben had not been able to get an explanation from the Lathams' rich and powerful friends—friends who'd circled the wagons, obviously seeing him as a kid, an intrusion, from the wrong side of the tracks.

Soon enough town rumors had surfaced that Abbie was seriously ill. Friends to whom Abbie had tearfully confided her "need for freedom" had suspected some kind of mental or emotional illness. A breakdown, perhaps. Why else would sweet Abbie Latham desert the love of her life? They'd seemed as much in the dark as Ben, and had tended to side with him and his outraged sense of abandonment.

When Ben had tried to find Abbie, he'd come up against Latham power. He'd been twenty-two at the time, about to graduate from college, still wet behind the ears in many ways, without money or connections. What chance had he stood against Latham influence? None. Grant and Celeste had never approved of him as a match for their only child. They'd always kept one eye on a good excuse to break the couple up.

When they'd left town with Abbie, they'd forced a split in spades, then executed one hell of a job covering their tracks.

Now, as police chief, Ben had resources. But he couldn't care less about Abbie Latham. Well, that wasn't exactly true. He wouldn't care less once he heard the truth from her own lips. He needed her to tell him what had gone wrong eight years ago. He needed to tell her he was disappointed in her gutless behavior. Then he could walk away. Forget her. For good.

Because he was over her.

Hauling his attention back to the present, he saw her standing next to Serena's car, and he nearly ran his cruiser into the ditch. He almost had to radio the rescue squad to jump-start his heart. To regain his usual self-control, he stopped on the shoulder a couple houses up from the old Arrondise place.

Abbie Latham was back in town. Why?

And why did he still feel that old physical jolt? Way after he'd gotten over her.

She stood talking to Serena, and he noted the marked difference between the two women. Serena was model beautiful, with a city sophistication that made a man edgy. Abbie had always been country wholesome, down-to-earth and approachable, with a vulnerability that made a guy want to protect her. As she stood in animated conversation with Serena, wisps of wavy chestnut hair escaped the yellow ribbon at the nape of her neck and formed a halo about her head, transforming her. Making her seem almost otherworldly. Remote and untouchable. The difference in her appearance eight years ago and now pulled at his insides before he pulled himself up short.

Where had she been for all those years?

Anger and hurt pride replaced admiration.

"Let's get this over with," he muttered to himself, throwing the cruiser in gear. He drove the short distance down the street and pulled up behind Serena's Volvo.

Serena's face lit up at the sight of him. He knew the Realtor would like to develop a relationship beyond friendship, but, pretty as she was, he couldn't bring himself to go in that direction. Even now, he had eyes only for Abbie.

What a crock.

Abbie Latham meant nothing to him, he reminded himself as he got out of the cruiser.

"Ben!" Serena fairly purred her welcome.

Abbie said nothing, her breath on this sunny winter day wreathing her slightly parted lips...lips red with the cold. Time rewound. It could have been the yesterday of eight years ago when he couldn't get enough of Abbie Latham's healthy glow, her energy, her huge capacity for love, those lips—

"Serena, could you give Abbie and me a couple minutes?" No use spinning his wheels with pleasantries. The more time he wasted the more time his emotions had for treachery.

"Of course." Hurt and confusion flickered in the Realtor's eyes. "I'll be inside."

As soon as Serena closed the cottage door behind her, Ben turned to Abbie. "Why did you leave, and why are you back?"

Abbie sucked in her breath, touched a tiny gold pin

on the shoulder of her coat. "I deserved that. But this isn't the place or time—"

"We don't need any more than a minute. Tell me right out, and I'll get out of your way. Were you pregnant?"

"Pregnant! Oh, my! If I'd been pregnant, you'd have been the first to know."

He was good at reading faces. The look of astonishment on hers told him he'd been way off base. "Then what? Other rumors had it you were sick."

She took a few seconds to compose herself. Finally she raised her chin, looked him directly in the eye. "I was sick, yes." He saw a strength he'd never associated with her before. "Very sick. That's why I left."

"So sick you couldn't have confided in me?" Frustration beat out concern. Why hadn't she told him? Why hadn't she let him help? He moved his mouth to speak, but the words came with great difficulty, sounded forced and rusty. "You couldn't have confided in your fiancé?"

"I'm sorry, Ben." Sadness drained color from her features. "I wanted to spare you."

"Spare me?" He shook his head in disbelief. "We were about to promise for better or for worse, in sickness and in health—"

"I'm not saying I'd do the same thing all over again. But I can't change the past. At the time, leaving seemed absolutely right."

"For whom?" Anger crackled in his words.

"I told you I made what I thought was the best decision at the time. For both of us." She folded her gloved hands tightly before her as if she might be nervous, but her regard never wavered. It captured him and wouldn't let him look away. "My parents and I decided I should make a clean break so you could get on with your life."

"Hah, your parents." Bitterness slipped out with the words, negating any explanation she might offer.

"Ben, please. I know how you feel about my parents—"

"I know how your parents felt about us. About me." That old wound began to fester.

"They weren't thinking about us eight years ago," she insisted. "They were thinking about getting the best possible medical help for their only daughter. For…a very serious illness."

Her words hit him like a slap. How petty he must seem, dredging up ancient history when she'd faced a serious illness. An ordeal she hadn't allowed him to share. An ordeal she still hadn't explained.

She looked healthy now. She'd come back. How sick could she have been?

He had to ask. "What kind—"

"Could we talk later? I owe you an explanation, Ben, but not now." She glanced at the cottage window, where a curtain fell back into place. "Serena is waiting…and, I sense, worrying." Abbie's gentle decisiveness and her consideration for Serena brooked no argument.

He didn't want to talk later. He'd wanted this conversation to explain everything and end any further need for talk. But, strange, once he'd started talking, he couldn't seem to stop.

"I'm sorry about your illness," he said, his voice gruff, but the sentiment genuine. With his words he detained her a moment longer, promising himself once he let her go, they'd have absolutely no need to get together again. "But you're okay?"

"I'm okay." She smiled, that same soft smile that could light up a room, that could turn his insides to mush.

Scowling, he resisted the mush. Too, he bit the urge to say that since she appeared in good health now, her breaking up with him had been for nothing after all. He needed to be a bigger man than that wisecrack.

"What brings you back to town?" He felt powerless to cut the conversation short, powerless to let her go. What was wrong with him? "The Christmas Prelude?" The small town's annual holiday events had become a winter tourist attraction. He hoped she'd come back only for a visit. A brief visit. He could avoid her for a brief visit.

"No." She tipped her head in an almost challenging gesture. "This morning I signed a contract as Point Narrows' librarian. I start work Monday."

"You what?" For the second time today, Ben felt as if the ground shimmied underneath his feet. He'd known about the library opening, but never in his wildest dreams had he imagined Abbie Latham coming home to fill it.

"Abbie!" Serena poked her head out of the cottage doorway. "I don't mean to interrupt—" her body language fairly screamed the opposite "—but I have another appointment at three o'clock."

"Of course. I'll be right in." Abbie extended her hand to Ben. "We'll talk later."

"No need." He pretended he didn't notice her

hand, her offer of—what? Pity? "We've said all we have to say."

"I don't think we've scratched the surface, Ben Chase." She skewered him with a quick, penetrating glance, then turned and hurried into the cottage, leaving him standing alone in the cold, with more questions than answers.

And all he'd come for was one straight answer.

A hint of her perfume lingered in the brittle air. Damn. After an eight-year absence, the woman's presence now enveloped him. But why should it rattle him when he was over her? Why should it kick his feet out from under him? Why leave him panting?

Since her departure he'd forged a life without her. Now she'd shown up again—a bad penny?—without forewarning. Her arrival meant nothing to him, or so he told himself.

He didn't want her anymore.

The gusts swirling in from the harbor seemed to whisper, "Liar."

He buttoned his coat against that ill wind, then wrenched the cruiser door open.

Having signed a lease on the cottage and phoned in an order for groceries, Abbie jingled a handful of newly acquired keys in her pocket as she set out to walk the short distance to the town square.

Ben's appearance had unsettled her. Out of necessity she'd thought she'd gotten over him. But after their brief meeting she'd needed to use the calming techniques she'd practiced all through her recovery. Rechanneling her emotions, she'd focused on her new job at the library, the thought of which both calmed and energized her.

The library. Soon to be her library.

Although Pat Spenser, the retiring librarian, had closed up until tomorrow, Abbie would take a couple after-hours today and then again tomorrow to acquaint herself with the collection. Next week she and Pat would work together to effect a smooth transition in services. The anticipation tingled clear down to Abbie's booted toes. She'd always wanted to be a small-town librarian. Here. Only ever here. In Point Narrows. Home.

She'd never stopped thinking of Maine as home. With an ocean-smoothed pebble as her touchstone, she'd used her memories of this seaside village to soothe and sustain her throughout the past eight years, throughout surgery, chemotherapy, radiation and subsequent remission.

Ah, joyous remission!

Abbie skipped along the narrow sidewalk. Life was good. To be alive, in fact, was a miracle for which she gave thanks daily.

She needed to make Ben understand her journey. Soon. As soon as she'd regained her equilibrium from his last visit. Because she'd learned not to take time for granted.

Inhaling, she felt the air form ice crystals in her nostrils. The sky, having turned gray, spit a raggedy snow, but not enough to cover much of anything. Mother Nature was going to have to hustle if she planned to blanket the village in white sometime in the upcoming week before Christmas.

Christmas in Point Narrows! Her parents, in a wonderful gesture of conciliation—oh, how upset they'd been with her decision to return to Maine—planned to join her for a few days. Abbie did a little roadside jig at the thought of being home, truly home, again.

"As I live and breathe! Abbie Latham!" An ancient pickup truck slowed to keep pace with her. An equally ancient Herbie Thurow hung out the driver's window. The truck wobbled back and forth across the double yellow line as Herbie concentrated on Abbie. "You're a sight for sore eyes!"

"You, too!" Abbie laughed with delight. Herbie's weather-lined face hadn't changed since she'd seen him last. "How've you been?"

"Can't complain. Seen Ben?"

Abbie refused to get upset over Herbie's question. High school and college sweethearts, Ben and she had been so inseparable for so long, it was natural some of the older residents would be curious about their relationship, past and present. If she reacted with dignity, the local curiosity should fade.

"Yes, I've seen Ben," she replied, trying to keep that pesky catch out of her voice. "He stopped by to say hello—" the fib made her clear her throat "—as Serena Hopkins was showing me the Arrondise place."

Surprise registered in Herbie's faded blue eyes. "You thinking of renting—"

An insistent honk interrupted the reunion. During the brief conversation an out-of-state luxury car had cruised up behind Herbie's truck. The driver, tailgating on the narrow two-lane road, honked a second time for good measure.

"Durned tourists," Herbie muttered, narrowing his

eyes to slits. "I gotta git. But you come see me some-time. I came out of retirement to work at the hard-ware."

"I've come out of a retirement of sorts, too," Ab-bie replied, raising her hand in a goodwill gesture toward the impatient occupants of the out-of-state car.

With an evil look in his rearview mirror, Herbie threw his pickup into gear, revved the engine, then accelerated sharply, leaving two strips of rubber on the road and two astonished tourists in his wake.

Abbie laughed aloud. Some things never changed. Like Herbie Thurow, eighty-something, "retired" drag strip king.

And Ben Chase. He hadn't changed. He was still as compelling as ever.

Now, why had Ben popped into her head as she'd been thinking about Herbie? And about Christmas with her parents. And her new job. Heavens, she'd been thinking about almost anything except Ben. But here he came, poking his way into her consciousness. Upsetting her well-maintained equilibrium.

Perhaps she couldn't help thinking of him because he'd always been tied up with her image of home.

But, having broken with him eight years ago, she didn't expect to pick up where they'd left off. No. Even though he deserved an explanation—that later talk she'd promised him—she hadn't come home for Ben. She'd come home because the pull of New En-gland had pulsed in her bloodstream. Because she'd constantly missed the smell of the North Atlantic. Missed the flame-bright Maine autumns. The clipped speech of the inhabitants. Snow. Being able to *walk* to the grocery store. Growing up, she'd never imagined living anywhere else.

Her health—emotional, mental and physical—demanded she return home.

Oh, but she and Ben needed to come to an understanding before she could restart her life here.

"I can't change the past and I can't control the future, Murphy," she said aloud, placing her gloved hand over her guardian angel, the gold pin her father had given her right after her diagnosis. "I can only manage what feels right today. And moving back to Point Narrows feels *right*. Ben will understand. I'll make him understand."

In a burst of optimism, she raised her arms to the heavens. "Murph, look! I'm spreading my wings!"

She felt light-headed. Even the now surly, lead-gray sky seemed beautiful to her. Besides, who could entertain gray thoughts when the town was decked out in holiday red and green?

The closer Abbie came to the center of town, the more lavish the decorations. Someone had looped garlands threaded with twinkling white lights around the Wee Scot's Gift Shop. The cod weather vane atop the Potters' barn sported a wreath around its fat, fishy middle. Enormous crocks of freshly cut holly surrounded a sign stuck in the church front lawn, announcing a Christmas tea tomorrow.

Abbie thrilled to all of it.

Entering the square, she waved to a group taking a picture in front of the town's traditional "tree"—a pyramid of lobster traps trimmed with ribbons and tufts of greenery.

Home. She was home. She'd earned the return, and nothing could spoil the mood.

Climbing the sloped sidewalk to the library, she dug deep in her pocket for the key. Even though the facility was closed, the wreath hung high on the weathered clapboards and the twinkling white lights in the windows gave the old facility an open appearance, a welcoming demeanor. Pat had even left a few inner lights on for Abbie. Only the temporary winter windbreak, hunched bleakly against the front door, looked out of sorts. Made of plywood and Plexiglas, the seasonal structure sheltered the entry and the bookdrop from the insistent northeast wind.

Abbie saw a large plastic laundry basket nestled between the bookdrop and the building itself. A yellow blanket protected the contents. Obviously someone didn't want a fine for returning damp or damaged books.

Suddenly the contents of the basket moved.

"Oh, dear, Murphy, not kittens or puppies. Not in this weather." Abbie hurried to the entrance.

When she stooped to lift the blanket she saw, not books, not kittens or puppies, but a heavily swaddled infant. On the underside of the faded but clean yellow blanket was pinned a note. It read, "Please take care of my son."

Chapter Two

"So you're saying this town's not big enough for the two of you?" On the dock behind his harborside home on the Leeward Road, Garrett Chase looked up from the lobster trap he was repairing.

"Oh, that would be real mature." Leaning against a pylon, Ben glowered at his younger brother.

"Then what are you saying?"

"Nothing more than Abbie's back. Of course we'll run into each other in a town this size." Ben picked up a scrap of wood and hurled it onto the outgoing tide. "I'm not happy about it, but it's no big deal. I'm sorry I brought it up."

"Forget her, Ben."

"I have." He wished it were so.

"She's trouble."

"I know."

"Besides," Garrett persisted, "I'm surprised her parents let their princess out of their sight."

"She's thirty years old."

"Once a rich little daddy's girl, always a rich little daddy's girl."

"You don't know the whole story."

"Do you?"

"I don't need to." Ben, never one for locker-room talk or gossip, didn't feel he had the right to pass around Abbie's scant explanation, not even to his own family. Especially to his own family, who'd loyally and vocally condemned her leaving. Defending Abbie's actions to the Chases might mean he cared. And he didn't. "I don't care."

Well, he did care that she was okay. No one in their right mind could remain impassive when they heard another had done battle with a serious illness. But that was the extent of his caring—one detached human being for another. Period.

He rammed his gloved hands under his armpits. Damn, but the day had turned raw.

Garrett flung the repaired trap on top of a stack, then turned his attention to another. "Well, I bet the whole story doesn't have the high-and-mighty Lathams recanting the belief their golden girl is too good for the likes of working-class Chases."

"Give it a rest, Garrett."

"You ready to swear Grant and Celeste didn't brainwash her into leaving you?" Ah, that old chestnut. His family had roasted it on more than one occasion.

"Maybe the whys are complicated." Ben smarted under Abbie's reluctance, even now, to come clean on the whys. He didn't buy her promise of a later explanation. "She left. That's the point. It's over and done."

"Why'd she come back?"

"She took the library position."

"There have to be thousands of libraries across the country. Why here?"

"I don't know." He didn't care. "Do I look like her keeper?"

Pausing in his repairs, Garrett cocked one eyebrow, stared hard at Ben. "Did you think to ask her why she came back?"

"Sure I asked her. But she was in the middle of looking at the Arrondise place, and Serena had another appointment—"

"What are you going to do about Serena?"

"There's nothing between Serena and me."

Garrett grinned. "Tell that to Serena."

"Maybe you ought to get more than basic cable." Ben cuffed his brother smartly on the shoulder. "Seems you're shy on entertainment, kid."

Ben's pager went off. Good. The best way to get his mind off Abbie's return was to throw himself into his work. "Gotta go."

"Saturday dinner's here," Garrett reminded him. "If you're not too busy sorting out your personal life."

Ignoring the jab, Ben dashed up the long, sloping backyard to his cruiser parked in the younger Chase's driveway.

The radio crackled as he checked in. "Oh, Ben! You just have to get over to the library. Abbie Latham called and she, like, found this little bitty baby who was totally *abandoned* with just a note and a few diapers—''

"Suki, slow down." Suki Zukerman had been the police dispatcher for a month now. Ben despaired of ever getting her to deliver messages according to code and protocol. "Is the baby with Abbie at the library now?"

"Yes, and it's a boy. Not more than a couple months old, Abbie says. And in really fine health, considering some good-for-nothing who calls herself a mother nearly stuffed him in the bookdrop—''

"Suki!"

"Yes, sir?"

"Call Abbie back. Tell her I'm on my way." He cut off the radio before Suki could overwhelm him with any more commentary.

An abandoned baby. Anger and an ancient hurt welled deep inside Ben. He'd been a castoff at twelve, and no amount of professional detachment would ever harden him to the plight of unwanted children. Grimly he set his mind to the task ahead.

Although it was only four-fifteen, dusk shrouded the town as he drove the short distance to the library. Streetlights had come on, as had many Christmas lights. Ah, the season of love for a little child. How ironic.

Christmas was always a difficult time for Ben. His mother had left before Christmas, and he could never understand why she'd gone to all the trouble of buying and wrapping the presents if she was going to leave. For good. Did she think if they each had a present, they wouldn't notice their mother was missing? Jonas didn't, because he wasn't even one, still a baby. But the other three were miserable, crying miserable. Ben couldn't cry. At twelve, he was expected to suck it up like a man, even after being dumped like someone's unwanted trash.

Suki had said this foundling was a baby, as Jonas had been. Perhaps they could get it into foster care before it felt the shock of abandonment.

Ben shook his head, trying to dislodge painful thoughts of the past. He concentrated instead on Janis McDougal, the social worker assigned to this area. After a hard day's work, she wouldn't be thrilled to get his call. But she'd cover gracefully. She loved kids that much. The area was lucky to have her.

He parked in the empty space marked Librarian and tried not to think about Abbie. Once he'd taken her statement and contacted Janis, Abbie could leave. Janis would take care of finding the baby a foster home.

He needed to think about finding the mother, about bringing her to justice. Truth and consequences.

With more force than necessary, he pushed open the door to the library.

Abbie stood in front of him, a startled look on her face. In her arms she cradled a sleeping infant. For a heartbreaking moment time dropped away, and Ben imagined he'd come home, and she'd been waiting for him. With their child. For some crazy reason fantasy had sunk its teeth in Ben and wouldn't let go.

"Who would do something like this?" she asked, shattering the spell.

Anger replaced fantasy. "I don't know. But we'll find out," he replied, automatically stepping to her side. "Does he seem all right?"

"Oh, he's beautiful." Abbie beamed, moving aside the blanket to reveal the tiny, pink-faced boy. "He has all his parts. I checked when I changed him. His snowsuit, creeper and blanket are all worn, but clean. I don't think he was abused or neglected."

"No. Just abandoned. Lucky kid." The sarcasm slipped out on a wave of disgust. Not at Abbie, but at the missing mother.

The sight of Abbie holding the baby moved Ben more than he cared to admit. In self-defense, he turned to the plastic laundry basket on one of the tables. "What else came with him?"

"A clean bottle, a can of formula, an extra creeper and three unused disposable diapers." She picked up a slip of paper from her desk and handed it to him. "And this note."

"Please take care of my son."

The loopy, anonymous scrawl taunted him, the *please* irking him most of all. Was it okay to dump your baby as long as you did it politely? Ben shook his head. Maybe he was being too harsh. In the note and the few extra supplies, this child already had a more personal legacy from his mother than the Chase kids had received from theirs.

"Ben?" Abbie's voice cut into his thoughts. "Do you suppose the mother's in trouble?"

"She will be. I promise you." Carefully sliding the note into his breast pocket, he reached for the phone on the desk.

Abbie tucked the baby more closely to her chest. "But maybe she's afraid or ill. She may need help."

"We have to help the innocent first." He punched

in the Social Services number. "We have to find this little guy a foster home."

"It might not be a clear case of innocence or guilt." Abbie rocked the baby in her arms and frowned. "Life isn't always black and white."

How naive could she be?

He held up his hand to discourage further conversation. The receptionist at Social Services picked up. "Janis McDougal," Ben said.

As he waited to be connected, his gaze locked on the sight of Abbie's lithe body released from the bulky overcoat she'd worn earlier in the day. A soft, butter-yellow sweater hugged all her curves, accented her titian coloring and made him break out in a sweat. A moss-green miniskirt over dark stockings made her shapely legs go on forever. He needed air. Holding the baby, she looked pure and sensual all at the same time. He knew he shouldn't stare. This was a professional interaction, plain and simple, but under the uniform he was still a man. And she was still a looker.

"Janis McDougal speaking."

"Janis, Ben Chase." He shook off all inappropriate thoughts. "We have an abandoned baby boy in need of an immediate foster home."

"I don't want to hear that, Ben." Janis's sigh skittered over the phone line. "It's a week before Christmas. We've placed as many kids as we possibly can. To put it bluntly, there's no room at the inn."

"I've never heard you say no."

"I'm not saying no. I'm merely saying we'll have to get creative."

"Meaning?"

"Could you—?"

"No!" He'd fostered one child for Janis in another emergency situation, and the letting go had nearly killed him. "I'm short staffed with Ned on sick leave. The town's crawling with tourists for the Prelude. I'm never home."

Janis let his excuses slide by without comment. "Who found the child?" she asked instead.

"The new librarian. The baby was left in a basket near the bookdrop."

"This librarian. Do you know her?"

"Yeah. Abbie Latham. We…went to school together."

"What's her situation? Married? Kids? Sensitive to the needs of the community? I guess I'm asking if you could vouch for her."

Janis and he had worked together on many—too many, if you thought of the kids—cases, from which they'd forged a solid, mutual trust. He knew the direction she was taking.

"I'd have to talk to her." He could vouch for Abbie's love of kids, but he wouldn't want to testify to her reliability. He'd been stung in that department.

"I'd want to talk to her, too, of course. A quick, gut-instinct interview." Janis made a sound as if shuffling papers. "Where are you?"

"The Point Narrows library." He watched Abbie as she prepared to feed a bottle to the now wakeful, now fussy baby. She performed the task as if she'd done it dozens of times before. The sight filled him with a longing he quickly squelched. He needed to get out of her disconcerting presence.

"Don't move," Janis ordered. "I have an errand in your direction and can be there in five minutes. If you vouch for Ms. Latham and I get a good feeling about her, perhaps we can work a temporary situation.''

''Such as?''

''See if she'd be willing to take the baby until we find the mother,'' Janis urged. ''Or, at least, until Monday when I *might* be able to find another home.''

''I'll talk to her.''

''And I'll bless you with a dozen homemade chocolate chip cookies,'' Janis promised. ''You're salt of the earth, Ben Chase.''

''Why do I give in to your flattery?''

''Because I'm one of the few who know how to work the teddy bear lurking beneath your tough-cop exterior. I'll be right over.''

It might be better all around if he just accepted responsibility for the baby. Then he wouldn't have to maintain any contact with Abbie. But he hadn't been lying about his extra work duties. He was rarely at home this frantic holiday season. With his community obligations, he couldn't spare time to take in this child—or time to deal with Abbie.

''Ben?'' Janis's voice prodded him from the other end of the line.

''I'll see what I can do.''

He hung up and wondered how to handle Janis's unusual request. Beyond his own concerns, he hadn't considered Abbie's. What were her circumstances? Unfortunately, to get the answer to that question, he needed to spend more time in her company than he'd intended when first responding to this call.

''Abbie,'' he began, ''I need to ask you a favor.''

When Ben called her by name, a tiny thrill ran

down Abbie's spine. She took a moment to make certain the baby was sucking the bottle before she looked up. She needed that much time to remind herself Ben and she were not here, together, alone, under personal circumstances. She mustn't show that his very presence excited her, brought back an old, half-forgotten yearning. She must focus on the baby's well-being.

When she did look up, she found herself staring into blue-gray eyes so familiar they made her heart constrict.

Ben's eyes were one of his attributes she'd never, ever forget. Even when he'd exuded macho swagger with his body language back in high school and college, his eyes always had spoken the inner truth. Sometimes that truth had revealed a young man more sensitive, more vulnerable than his outward posture.

Surprisingly, such was the case now. Ben looked unsure of himself.

"A favor?" she asked.

"It looks as if Monday will be the earliest Social Services can find a foster home for the baby."

Abbie smiled down at the little boy feeding greedily. A warm contentment blanketed her. "Well, I'll just have to keep him till then." She looked up at Ben. "So what's the favor?"

"That was the favor." He bristled. "Perhaps you need to give it more thought."

"Why?"

The muscle along his jaw twitched. "Because your track record for staying in town isn't the best."

Glancing at the baby, she determined not to respond to Ben's low blow, for she could understand his prickly behavior. She'd left him eight years ago with an explanation forged on half-truth. There was no glossing over the fact. Moreover, his own mother...well, the child Abbie now held had to push some very painful buttons.

"I'm staying," she said with calm conviction. "I have a job, and I want to be a contributing member of the community. If taking in this baby would help, I'd be honored to do it." She didn't mention the infant filled a need for her, as well.

"Are you strong enough?" He scowled. "Physically, I mean."

Tension seeped into the room.

"Yes, I'm strong enough." She contemplated telling him her whole story just to clear the air. But her story needed a delicate unfolding so as not to look like a plea for pity. Now wasn't the time. Not when the past seemed doubly explosive with the symbolism of one tiny abandoned baby. "I can handle Baby. In fact, he's just what the doctor ordered."

"What about a boyfriend?"

"Boyfriend?"

"Fiancé. Significant other. Someone who might see this added responsibility as an intrusion."

"I'm quite unattached." She felt herself blush and quickly covered by placing the baby on her shoulder for a thorough round of burping. "And next week in the library will be a transition week. An apprenticeship of sorts. I'm sure it can be flexible." She hazarded a glance at him. "Did I pass the interview?"

"Janis McDougal has the final say. She'll be here in a couple minutes." He looked as if the social worker couldn't get here fast enough.

"But you don't approve my taking the baby."

"I didn't say that." He paced the one-room library. "The Abbie I used to know was warm and compassionate and loved kids. She'd have made a terrific foster mother." He stopped, his expression hard. "Frankly, I don't have a clue as to who you are anymore."

"I haven't changed. If anything, a brush with…a severe illness makes you more of who you were. It distills your essence." She felt a quick warmth spread across the baby's diapered front. "Goodness, Baby! Did you even bother to digest your dinner?"

The corner of Ben's mouth twitched. "Here." Reaching into the laundry basket, he pulled out two spare diapers. "Use the second one as a shield. He's a boy. He's saved some in reserve for the public fountain."

The outer door in the library's windbreak opened.

"That'll be Janis," he said with obvious relief, moving to meet the social worker. "She may need help. She usually brings an infant car seat."

Abbie gently laid the baby on the desk blotter, then with a feeling approaching awe, removed his legs from the creeper. "What fat toes!" she exclaimed.

The baby stared at her.

"Did your mommy play 'This Little Piggy'?"

As she tickled first one toe and then another, his eyes grew round as saucers. When she had his whole attention, she deftly changed his diaper. Before snapping the creeper she planted a noisy raspberry on his baby-smelling tummy and could have sworn she saw him smile.

"Good work."

She turned to see a pleasant, silver-haired woman standing next to Ben. "I'm Janis McDougal."

"Abbie Latham." She scooped the freshly changed infant into her arms. "And this is Baby."

"He seems very comfortable with you."

"And why wouldn't he be? I have food, clean diapers and an endless supply of nursery rhymes."

"May I?" Janis reached for the child. "Ben says you're willing to become a foster mom until we can find a less temporary home." In an unobtrusive way, she examined the little guy.

"Yes. Are you willing to have me?"

"I am, yes. Call it first impressions." She turned to Ben. "And you?"

"Yes." Whereas he spoke with conviction, his eyes held a guarded willingness.

"Good. Because I have a request." She looked from Ben to Abbie. "We're coloring outside the lines here. Ben is already on our books as a foster father. I'd feel better if he kept close contact in a supervisory capacity."

"Janis—"

"As part of your rounds, Chief. Abbie will be the primary caregiver. You just have to look in from time to time."

"I would have taken him myself," Ben protested, "but I'm swamped."

"It's only for a weekend," Abbie urged. "I could use the backup."

Ben turned to Janis. "You're sure you can get a less temporary home by Monday?"

"I'll try my best." Without looking at Ben, Janis handed the baby to Abbie. "I didn't have time to bring the paperwork. It was either that or a car seat. Why don't the three of us meet tomorrow morning to tie things up?''

"One-forty Leeward Road," Abbie said. "It's a Victorian cottage you can't miss."

"I think you two can handle it." Ben looked as if he needed air. "I need to start an investigation."

"I'd like to hear your strategy for finding the mother. And the plan for after you've found her. That means we need you at our meeting tomorrow." Janis shot him a look that brooked no argument. "I'll bring the sticky buns."

"You are one determined woman, Janis Mc-Dougal." Ben shook his head. "Nine o'clock. I can give you fifteen minutes." He turned to Abbie. "I'll install the car seat. I'm going to need the laundry basket, cans of formula and spare bottle. To dust for prints. Before you go home, stop at the store for extras."

"I walked."

"Janis?" A stricken look on his face, Ben appealed to the now retreating social worker.

"I'm late! You're the first of three stops." She gave a backward wave. "Be a dear, Ben..."

The door swung shut before Ben could scrape his chin off the floor.

"Would you give me a lift?" Abbie ventured.

His features presented a formidable stoniness, an impassive professionalism. "Sure."

He might have said yes, but his whole demeanor returned to no. Standing, one large hand resting on his lean hip, the other relaxed by a well-muscled thigh, he appeared every inch the image of law and order. Cool. Detached. "Whenever you're ready."

"Would you hold the baby while I gather up his things?" She didn't let his scowl or his cop's demeanor deter her. She simply handed the little guy over.

Ben stiffened as his hand covered hers in the transfer, but Abbie knew his discomfort came from touching her, not the baby. Ben had long experience with child rearing. When his mother had left, Ben had helped his father raise the other four siblings. He'd cared for them with more than a sense of duty. He'd acted with love. And he'd only ever let Abbie know how abandoned he'd felt.

And hadn't she, in turn, abandoned him? The thought gave her pause.

Why had she expected, after leaving him with a false explanation those eight years ago, she could waltz back into town with an apology and a hope they could be friends? Had she been totally selfish in her return?

The questions made her waver in her determination to reclaim Point Narrows as home, until she began to gather up the meager baby supply of clothing and blankets, leaving the rest for Ben's investigation. She'd returned to Maine for her own well-being, yes, but had found this child needing her, if only for a weekend. A sign, if she'd ever received one.

As she picked up the tiny blue snowsuit lying on top of her own overcoat, the light caught Murphy pinned to her coat's shoulder, and made the golden angel twinkle as if he were winking, as if he sought to remind her that she could find a way to be selfish and selfless at the same time.

It was the season of miracles, he seemed to say.

When Abbie turned to Ben, she found him engrossed in holding the baby. His large hands dwarfed the infant's body, but he held the child with a gentleness and an assurance that made her ache. She'd never doubted he'd make a terrific father. The ache near her heart deepened as she thought of the children they would never have.

But no one ever conquered the world with thoughts of what couldn't be. Although so much seemed beyond control in her life, Abbie knew she held the reins to her attitude. Breathing deeply, she looked at the baby and turned her ache upside down until it became a smile. This little boy's need was greater than her own. She would nurture him one day at a time and consider the act a serendipitous gift. A two-way gift.

She laid the snowsuit on the table. Moving to dress the infant in the garment, Ben brushed by her so closely she smelled the wool scent of his officer's jacket mixed with the tang of crisp winter air and an elusive whiff of masculinity, edgy and raw. Her traitorous mind instantly called up the memory of snuggling deep into those familiar scents many years ago. Of football games. And movies. And study dates on lumpy sofas—

"There's snow forecast for tonight." Ben zipped up the infant's snowsuit and snapped Abbie back into the present. He handed the now drowsy boy to Abbie. "Once you get home, don't go anywhere."

"I wasn't planning to. But what if we forget something at the store?"

The muscle along his jaw jumped. "Call me." The wary look in his eyes said he'd come, but he wouldn't like it.

She cleared her throat, uncomfortably aware of his masculine bulk in close quarters. He was tall and proudly erect and handsome as a granite facing. Stone-cold handsome.

He'd always been a physical standout, even back in the days of high school and college sports. Back when they'd been in love and inseparable. Now, upon closer inspection, his athletic good looks showed a ragged edge in the tiny lines that fanned out from the corners of his eyes, in the tense set of his mouth.

"I'll try not to wear out the option," she said, picking up the library keys from the desk. She'd be a fool to place herself in Ben's disconcerting company any longer than necessary.

He reached for the keys. "I'll lock up."

When he wrapped his fingers around hers, Abbie started at his touch. It had been eight long years, yet her memory had preserved to perfection the feel of his callused fingers, the dry warmth of his skin, the strength of muscle and sinew. He exuded both an aura of highly evolved power and unsettling animal magnetism. With his fingers around hers for only a few seconds, she felt her resistance buckle in the face of the attraction she still felt for him.

Abbie caught her breath at the sensuality in his regard. Did he feel a fraction of the attraction she felt? Why had she thought her emotions could handle such a reunion?

Clutching the baby, she searched for neutral conversation.

"How difficult will it be to find the mother?"

Picking up the empty laundry basket and the car seat, he ushered her into the foyer. "Like looking for the proverbial needle in a haystack."

"Poor little one." Kissing the infant's forehead before covering him totally with the blanket, she thought of her own loving parents. "You need your mother."

Ben opened the outer door. "Maybe he's better off without her," he replied, his words rimed with an unmistakable frost.

Abbie opened her mouth, but found no words to respond. She stood frozen as an icy blast of air set loose by the unlatched door swirled around her, bringing with it the pungent scent of evergreen from the beribboned holiday spray on the door and fat snowflakes that flitted like winter moths about the entryway light.

"You worry about the baby," Ben added. "I'll take care of the mother." A sudden shadow passed over his eyes, giving Abbie the impression he'd slammed shut a storm door to his inner emotions and had bolted it firmly against her.

"Maybe I could provide some insight into the mother," she insisted. "I know what helplessness feels like."

"You had plenty of help at your fingertips." He shot her a chilling look. "You only had to ask."

Sadly, she remembered how the younger Ben had coped with those who'd tried to do him wrong, or those he'd perceived had set out to hurt him. He never stooped to revenge. He merely cut them out of his life. Absolutely. And he must view her as having committed an unforgivable wrong against him by leaving eight years ago. The way he looked at her now, as if she were a stranger, clearly said he did.

"The baby," he said, nodding toward the parked cruiser.

Yes, all else paled beside the baby's welfare. With care, so as not to slip on the snow dusting the pavement, she made her way to the patrol car while Ben locked up the library.

She waited in silence for him to help her with the car door. When he at last stood beside her, her reticence slipped. "I'm sorry," she offered. "I'm sorry that what's between us is getting in the way of moving on. I want to explain."

Only the streetlight illuminated them. Glittering flakes of snow danced in magical patterns and stuck to their clothing like quickly disappearing sequins. Time stood still, and for a moment the possibility he'd accept her apology hung in the air.

"There's nothing between us, Abbie," he said, opening the car door. "Not a thing."

With his brusque declaration, he annulled all they'd ever shared.

His words cut deep. She hadn't come back to Point Narrows for a renewed relationship. She'd wanted a sense of balance, of home, of rootedness, knowing full well she'd have to bring closure to her past relationship with Ben. She hadn't counted on him trying to erase any acknowledgment of their former bond.

Holding the baby tightly to her, and holding back tears, she got into the cruiser.

Chapter Three

Seeing the hurt in Abbie's eyes, Ben felt like a creep. Without apologizing, however, he double-checked that she'd buckled the baby properly into the car seat he'd secured in the back of the cruiser, then walked around to the driver's side. Why should he have to apologize for speaking the truth?

Nothing resembling a relationship remained between them. In choosing to shut him out eight years ago, she'd given up her right to speak the word *relationship* where the two of them were concerned. Sure, the baby tied them together for the weekend. But Janis McDougal would act as a buffer.

He slid behind the wheel. "Buckle up," he reminded her, that old protective instinct rising to the surface.

She fumbled in her efforts to free the safety harness. Without a second thought, he reached across to help her. In pulling the belt from its restraint near the window, he grazed her cheek with the backs of his fingers. Her soft skin seared his senses. With an intake of breath, he secured the belt in its lock, then turned to start the car.

Why, if he'd gotten over her, did she still have the power to move him?

He absolutely needed to minimize his contact with her. And here he'd promised Janis he'd supervise the temporary foster situation, had agreed to meet with the two of them tomorrow, had told Abbie to call him if she needed help over the weekend. What had he been thinking?

"Branson's store okay?" he asked, reining in his irritation. "It's closest." He needed to stop, shop and get her home. Out of his cruiser. Out of the range of his overworked senses.

"I'm sure they'll have the basics," she replied with a cool calm that hinted she, too, was struggling to create distance between them.

Good. They'd need to look cool, calm and unattached as they shopped together—with a baby, no less—under the prying eyes of Point Narrows' residents. And under the certain disapproval of Margot, his sister, who was scheduled to work the evening shift register. He hoped she hadn't signed in yet.

Perhaps, if Abbie shopped on her own, he could begin to ask some questions concerning the disappearing mother. That way he could get a jump start on the investigation, and Abbie and he wouldn't look as if they were *together*.

"I would have called Branson's to have them send

over the supplies,'' Abbie said, a note of apology in her words, ''but they cut off delivery at five.''

''That's okay.'' It wasn't, but he'd live.

Ben drove the short distance to Branson's, thankful for yet uncomfortable with the silence that hung in the patrol car. He parked near the entrance.

''I can run in and pick up a few things,'' he offered hopefully. ''You could stay in the cruiser. Keep warm.''

''No.'' She brightened. ''I want to do this. It makes me feel needed. Alive.''

He was struck by the energy she put into the word *alive*. Was struck, too, by how she made a mundane errand seem so appealing.

He harrumphed to himself, thinking this supposedly simple task might prove tricky. For one thing, as he made his way around the car to help her and the baby, he noted with chagrin the small general store was filled as usual with people stopping by after work. Damn. Folks around here were always on the lookout for a long tale to enliven a short winter day.

Then again, perhaps more crowded was better than less. Maybe people intent on finding that quick and easy supper at the deli counter wouldn't have time or energy to wonder about the police chief, the new librarian and a baby.

Right.

''Well, now, lookee here!'' Herbie Thurow's voice caught Ben off guard as he held the cruiser door open for Abbie. ''Reunited less than twenty-four hours and it appears you two have been busy.'' Herbie issued his signature braying laugh.

So much for slipping in and out unnoticed.

Ben kept his cool even as Herbie peered over his shoulder in an attempt to get a better look at Abbie and the baby.

Might as well begin his investigation. "Herbie, were you working the gas pumps at the hardware this afternoon?"

"Sure was."

"Then you had a front-row seat. Did you happen to see someone leave that plastic laundry basket—" he indicated the one in the back seat "—by the library bookdrop? Sometime between the time Pat closed at three and four?"

"Can't say I did. What was in it?"

"This baby," Abbie said. "This baby whom I need to get out of the cold," she added pointedly.

"Oh, my. A mystery." Scratching his head, Herbie fairly danced ahead of Abbie. "You mean to say someone abandoned the child?"

"Yes." Ben shielded Abbie and the baby as a group of teenagers flung themselves out of the store in a laughing, heedless mass. "And we need to find the mother."

"In Branson's?" Herbie stepped aside to let Abbie enter first.

"No, Herbie." Abbie chuckled. "We need to pick up a few supplies and get him home. He's had a big day."

"Home?" Herbie's eyes grew wide. "You two planning to foster him together?"

"No!" Ben and Abbie spoke in unison.

"Abbie's volunteered to take him—to *her* place— until Janis McDougal can find a more permanent home."

"Pity." Herbie shook his head. "You three present quite the family picture."

"We're getting off track here." Ben reached for a shopping basket. "So long, Herbie. If you remember anyone near that bookdrop, let me know." He muscled between Abbie and the older man, then guided Abbie and the baby down the narrow aisle toward the infant supply section. Glancing back over his shoulder, he saw the nosy codger turn in search of an audience.

Why did this attention bother him? He was only doing his job. For the baby. For Janis. For the community. Abbie was a minor detail. Family picture indeed.

With an amused roll of her eyes, Abbie peeked under the yellow blanket. "How can this baby sleep through Herbie Thurow?"

"Babies have their own agenda." Glad for an excuse to turn the conversation back to the infant, Ben reached for several cans of formula, a six-pack of baby bottles, a carton of wipes and an economy-sized package of disposable diapers. A veteran of Janis's foster children as well as his own nephews and nieces, he didn't hesitate in his choices. "You'll discover how different that agenda is from yours about three in the morning."

She cast him a look filled with mischief. "Can I call you then?"

"Only if he asks for me by name." He suddenly felt self-conscious, standing in the store aisle shopping for baby supplies with a woman he'd once wanted to marry. *Once.* That was the key word. "This should do it for now. Janis will bring extras tomorrow, along with some more clothes and blankets for the baby. She's good at that sort of thing."

"You're not so bad yourself." Abbie shifted the baby in her arms. "Thanks."

"It's for the baby."

"I know." Her look said she might read more into his assistance if he'd just give her the chance. He wouldn't. "Let's check out before Herbie calls the *National Enquirer.*"

He hadn't counted on a former classmate, Denise Potter, ambushing them.

"Abbie Latham? Is it really you? And is this your baby?" Denise could talk rings around Herbie.

Raising the shopping basket, Ben caught Abbie's eye. "Meet you at the register. Don't be long."

Don't be long. He sounded like her husband.

Frustrated, he made his way to the front of the store. How the hell was he supposed to begin an investigation with a package of disposables under his arm? With the curious stares pointed in his direction, he felt *he* was under the microscope. Just let him get Abbie out of here, get the three of them out from under Point Narrows' scrutiny, and then he could get back on track. Professionally.

Glancing back over his shoulder at Abbie, he plunked the basket on the register's empty belt.

"What do you think you're doing, Benjamin Lucas Chase?" The all-too-familiar voice simmered with vexation.

Swiveling, he looked into the flashing eyes of the one cashier he'd hoped to avoid.

A year younger than Ben, his only sister, Margot, acted as if she were the elder, the protector. Raised in a family of five males, she was a spitfire, headstrong and unforgiving. At twenty-nine she'd discouraged more suitors than Ben could recall. Her sharp tongue made mincemeat of them all. Moreover, she was the one Chase who'd fiercely sworn she'd never forgive Abbie Latham for deserting her big brother. To add exclamation point to the vow, she'd declared she'd scratch Abbie's eyes out if she ever dared show her face in town.

A public market wouldn't deter Margot.

Ben set his jaw. He hadn't started the day with any intention of defending Abbie Latham, but his sister's antagonism put him on the defensive.

Ben chose his words carefully. "I'm on duty, Margot."

"With *her* tagging after you? What ill wind blew that bit of trash into town?" His sister narrowed her eyes and jutted her chin in Abbie's direction. As luck would have it, Abbie was distracted by a small crowd headed up by Denise Potter and Herbie Thurow.

"Watch your mouth." Ben threw Margot a pointed look. "Abbie's taken the library position."

"I heard as much. Didn't quite believe she'd have the nerve."

Ben pushed the baby supplies along the belt. "Could I get a little service, please?" He loved his difficult sister dearly, but he'd just as soon avoid a public airing of an old private discussion.

Margot ran the formula over the scanner. "What's going on here, Ben?"

"An abandoned baby. Abbie found him on the library steps this afternoon. Social Services won't have a place for him until Monday."

"Ah, yes and Saint Abbie, back in town from her own disappearing act, stepped in to pick up the slack. A real Mother Teresa." Margot made a face. "What a show."

"Pull in your claws." He wasn't thrilled Abbie had been the one to find the infant, but he never doubted the sincerity of her motives. "Cattiness doesn't suit you. Didn't I raise you better?"

"It's because you took care of me, big brother, I feel the need to return the favor."

"I can take care of myself, thank you very much."

"Is there a reason this line isn't moving?" An out-of-towner—a weekender clutching a bottle of merlot—scowled at Margot.

Margot smiled sweetly, always a sign of impending disaster. "I'm thinking of closing this register—"

"You'll do no such thing," Ben cautioned. "Ring. I'll bag." He reached for paper.

"So…she engineered you into shopping for her." Margot turned the price display so he could see the total. "How cozy."

"I suggest you buy a bag of chocolates on your break, sis." Reaching for his cash, he shook his head. "Your tongue could do with a little sweetening."

"And you could do with a refresher course in ancient history." She flipped him the receipt. "We'll talk at Saturday dinner."

"Which will be here sooner than any of us think," groused the man with the merlot.

"Hmmm…" With a glint in her eye, Margot turned to her next victim.

Although Ben pitied the man, he'd make good cover while Ben ushered Abbie and the baby out of the store. He told himself he was defending the baby. Not Abbie.

As soon as Abbie saw Ben bagging their purchases, she extricated herself from Point Narrows' curious citizens, who, it seemed, included the total residential census. Their noise level had reached that of a town meeting. It was past time to go. Amid the questions and comments, the baby woke and began to cry. She sympathized. It had been a long day, and she herself felt emotionally fatigued.

Across the store, Ben stood like an island of strength and relief. Unfortunately, she needed to wade through this sea of overwhelming interest and speculation to get to him.

"Give me a call if you need anything," Denise Potter insisted. "Anything at all."

All this commotion couldn't be good for the baby. In a rush of maternal instinct, Abbie nodded at Denise, pasted a smile on her lips, then, clutching the little boy tightly to her, pushed her way through the onlookers to Ben.

He appeared equally anxious to get out of the store, yet said nothing to her on the way to the car. His tight-lipped silence spoke volumes of discontent. Was she the source of his upset? Or did the animated exchange between his sister and him have something to do with it?

The relative isolation of the cruiser's interior came as a welcome change, even if she had traded a dozen inquisitive neighbors for one squalling infant and one taciturn adult, both male and both unhappy.

"He appears to have only two settings," she noted, glancing into the back seat where the baby lay buckled in the car seat, flailing his arms in infant outrage. "Off and On."

She could say the same for Ben. He now smoldered in the Off mode while the shrieking child gave On a heightened meaning.

"They sense confusion." Ah, the sphinx spoke. "Maybe the motion of the car will settle him down."

"Maybe he misses his mother." She reached into the back to stroke her new charge. "I've been thinking." It wasn't easy speaking over the distressed tyke's cries, but she needed to talk to Ben about the mother, because earlier he'd not wanted to, a reluctance that bespoke a counterproductive antagonism. "I think the mother loved her baby and wanted to keep him—"

"How can you say that? She abandoned him outside on a winter day." Ben's mood didn't get any rosier.

"Yes. But she left him out of the wind, in a well-traveled area where someone was certain to find him. And fairly quickly. Although the library was closed, Pat knew I was coming in and had left some lights on. It looked as if we were open, or at least working after-hours."

The infant settled somewhat with the motion of the cruiser.

"This is no newborn, Ben. He must be a couple months old. He's in good health. The mother cared for him this long. And although his belongings are few, they're clean. And she made certain to put extras in the basket, along with a plea to take care of her son. That sounds like someone who loves this child."

"You're reaching, Abbie."

"I have a hunch about this. Call it woman's intuition."

"Do you happen to have a hunch as to the mother's identity?"

"No. But I did learn something in the store. Something that might be helpful."

"Such as?"

"Denise Potter said when she was gassing up at M & M Hardware late this afternoon she saw three teenagers around the library door."

"Why would Denise make note of them?"

"Because her own daughter's in high school. Denise says the high schoolers use the facility a lot. But these kids looked new to the area. She almost called out to tell them the library would reopen Saturday morning, but Herbie sidetracked her." Abbie tickled the baby's feet through his snowsuit. "Denise appears to be Point Narrows' unofficial mother hen."

"That's putting it mildly." The corner of Ben's mouth twitched. "Did Denise say what these kids looked like?"

"She couldn't tell. They were bundled pretty heavily. But she thought there were two girls and a boy. While the girls were at the door, checking the schedule, presumably, the boy stayed in the car."

"Car? Did Denise note the make?"

"Some sporty little two-door compact. Black. Bumper stickers all over it. She noticed it mostly for the irony."

"Meaning?"

"The kid driving couldn't have been more than sixteen, barely old enough to make minimum wage, but his car was newer and in better shape than hers.

And she works full-time as a postal carrier. She said the irony got to her.''

He scowled.

''What's wrong?''

''Nothing.'' He pulled the cruiser into her cottage's gravel drive. ''I might as well deputize you right now.''

She couldn't tell if he was joking or upset.

''While I was buying diapers,'' he explained, ''you managed to start my job for me.''

''Are you angry?''

''No.'' He shut off the ignition, then turned to look at her. ''As Denise would say, the irony got to me.''

His steady gaze unsettled her. ''Are you coming in?'' she asked, surprised that he'd turned off the patrol car.

''Unless you're planning on making several trips.'' He indicated the baby in the car seat and the bags of supplies. ''I'll help you get the little guy settled in.''

''Good. I hadn't finished talking to you about the mother.''

''Ah, your hunches as to her maternal instincts.'' His words bore an unsympathetic edge.

''Please, remember that nothing is ever wholly as it seems.'' She referred to more than this baby's missing mother.

Staring at her, he opened his mouth as if to speak, then caught himself. While his eyes were full of unasked questions, his rigid body language told of his reluctance to voice them

''You want me to go easy on a woman who's abandoned her baby?'' He kept the topic on the baby and its mother, but Abbie would have wagered the questions he wanted to ask were about her. About him and her. Personal and painful questions.

"I want to make certain you use restraint and understanding when you eventually deal with this woman."

He turned a sharp glance on her. "All I want is justice."

"All I want is justice tempered with compassion."

"Why should you care?"

"I empathize with people who face daunting odds."

Her statement seemed to put him off balance. "Let's get this baby out of the cold," he said, the set of his broad shoulders unyielding.

Unstrapping the car seat, then making her way carefully up the front walk, Abbie wondered at the changes in her life since she'd left this little house only hours ago. Who would have thought she'd return with a baby and her former lover? Murphy, her guardian angel, would say a heightened awareness of being present in life led to all kinds of surprises.

Two large boxes with the groceries she'd ordered earlier sat on the doorstep. "I'll bring those in." Once again, Ben took the key from her hand and opened the door. "Is the house livable?"

"Oh, yes. But not what you'd call modern or convenient. The heirs haven't cleared it out yet." Abbie chuckled. "It looks as if Lily Arrondise still lives here."

Ben flicked on the hall light to expose a house straight out of the Victorian era. Or the Addams family. Red velvet, dark hand-carved moldings, and tas-

sels—lots of tassels—dominated the decor, along
with knickknacks on every available surface.

"You can't stay here with a baby," Ben insisted.

"Of course I can."

"It's not practical."

"If it were, it would lose some of its charm."

"I'm not even sure it's sanitary."

"For heaven's sake, Ben. Serena had a cleaning
crew go through when she listed it."

"You'll lose the baby amid all these—" he picked
up a ceramic cherub who'd been set to cavort on the
staircase "—what are they called?"

"Dust catchers." Resisting the urge to wink, she
smiled up at him. "But the baby's not crawling, is
he? And for all we know he'll be visually stimulated
by Lily's belongings."

As if on cue, the baby awoke and stared in openmouthed rapture at the profusion of *things.* "You
see," Abbie countered. "He loves it." She marched
toward the kitchen. "I could use a cup of herbal tea.
How about you?"

He could use a couple stiff pain relievers. Or a
rough one-on-one game of b-ball. Or a week's vacation someplace warm and far away. Herbal tea
wouldn't touch the tension headache Abbie's return
had precipitated.

He watched her walk away from him, the self-
assured click of her boot heels on the hardwood floor
playing a syncopated tag with the clanking of the
steam radiators. He looked at the narrow, crooked
staircase lined with bric-a-brac and thought it would
be no easy task to maneuver those treads alone, not
to mention with a babe in arms.

"Abbie!" He hauled the two boxes of groceries off the doorstep and into the foyer. Then, loaded with the baby supplies, he took off after her. "Branson's has a studio apartment over the store." He knew about it because he was considering moving for the winter out of the drafty fish house he'd been renovating. "Very modern. Very open. Very accessible. And close to the center of things. I'm sure Serena could work a swap."

"Whatever for?" Abbie looked up from the kitchen table where she'd laid the baby and was now taking off his snowsuit. "I saw the studio. Boring. Baby and I will be perfectly happy here." A fleeting melancholy expression clouded her features. "Besides, by the time he's crawling and into mischief, he'll be gone. You're forgetting the situation's temporary."

"Temporary or not, I'd worry about you and an infant in this white elephant." To his own ears he sounded disloyal. He loved this place. At the same time, he noted a lack of smoke detectors. Had the building ever had a fire inspection? What the hell was the wiring like? It was one thing to want to take the house over as a handyman's special, and another thing to bring a baby—

"You'd worry about me?" Abbie cocked her head.

"Of course I would." Setting the supplies on the counter, he scowled. "I vouched for you to Janis McDougal. This is a highly unorthodox situation to begin with." Although Janis could have no idea how unorthodox. "The baby's safety is my top priority."

"And mine." She dandled the boy in front of her. "But we have electricity, and we have heat, and we have running water," she said in singsong as if reciting a nursery rhyme. The baby cooed. "And we're going to have one terrific weekend until Uncle Ben can find your mommy."

Uncle Ben, indeed.

Irritated, he stalked out of the room to retrieve the remaining two boxes of groceries. Abbie was treating this as a lark. She didn't seem to understand the seriousness of the situation. Before he left her for the night, he'd have to check the house thoroughly. For all he knew, the attic had raccoons.

As he hefted the boxes, he caught himself mentally. Serena would say he had his nose out of joint because she'd found a tenant for the cottage and it wasn't him.

He quickly dispelled that notion. This wasn't about squatter's rights. This was about a foundling's well-being.

Yeah, right.

When he reentered the kitchen and deposited the grocery boxes alongside the baby supplies, Abbie handed the pink-cheeked child to him. "I'll make tea. I haven't figured out how to do it one-armed yet."

"Another reason why the studio over the store would be better," he pointed out, taking the energetically kicking baby. "If you got in a fix, someone's always downstairs. Margot, for instance."

"Oh, yes! Your sister, from the look she threw me earlier, would just love to help out!" She pulled an antique teakettle from the cupboard.

He felt embarrassed that Abbie had noticed Margot's animosity. "She's good with kids," he replied from a sense of family loyalty. "Maybe I should have asked her to take him."

"She works."

"Or Serena."

A curious look crossed Abbie's face. It appeared he'd challenged her in some way. "I certainly can handle a baby for a weekend."

Funny, but she looked as if she could handle anything she set her mind to.

"I wasn't questioning your abilities." As a familiar odor assailed him, he wrinkled his nose. "Our boy needs a change."

She laughed. "Why do you think I volunteered to make tea?"

Just like old times, she'd zinged him.

He suppressed a chuckle as he remembered how she'd always played these silly turnabout jokes on him. Had always guided him away from negative thoughts or confrontation, nudged him back into the positive with her gentle humor. She'd always seen the light, not the dark.

Once, in fact, she'd been the light of his existence. Unfortunately for his heart, that time seemed like yesterday.

What was he doing, letting her back into his thoughts?

"Would you at least empty one of those brown bags?" he asked, trying to keep his voice devoid of the emotions roiling inside him. "I'll use it as a changing pad."

"How resourceful." She flashed him a grin. "You could start your own helpful-household-hints column."

He resisted the attraction her grin generated. "I want to see where you plan to let this baby sleep."

"What's wrong with one of the drawers in the

chest next to my bed?'' She handed him an empty paper bag.

''Is the room sufficiently warm? Are there drafts?''

''I don't really know.'' She moved lightly about the kitchen, making tea, heating formula, putting away groceries. She looked so domestic, so *right* in this cottage. Just as they'd envisioned eight years ago. ''When I made my inspection, it wasn't with an eye to taking care of an infant. But we'll adapt. Yankee ingenuity.'' She grinned at him again.

To deflect her warm smile, he bent his head and concentrated on changing the soiled diaper. As the baby waved his arms and gurgled, Ben's heart caught. Maybe Abbie was right about the mother loving her child. The little boy seemed healthy and happy and trusting.

Why, then, would any woman in her right mind abandon him?

Why did a person abandon a loved one?

''The tea's steeping,'' Abbie announced. ''Do you want to check out the sleeping quarters to make certain I won't freeze this child?''

''Let's clear the knickknacks off the stairwell first. They're a menace.''

''No need.'' With a proprietary gesture, she lifted the freshly diapered baby from the table. ''There's a back staircase—straight and uncluttered—that leads to a bedroom right over the kitchen.'' Scooping up the bottle of warmed formula, she led the way.

He couldn't help but notice how easily she handled the baby, but he definitely pushed aside the thought that she would have made a terrific mother. Mother to *their* children. Entertaining such an outdated idea could prove dangerous.

Ascending the staircase with the baby in her arms, Abbie welcomed the buffer the child created between Ben and her. Actually, between Ben and the attraction she still felt for him. Of course, if there were no baby, Ben wouldn't be here. As he'd made perfectly clear, there was no longer anything between them. A true statement, a safe situation, but somehow sad, she thought.

At the landing, the stairwell opened up into a small sleeping garret with two dormer windows, a single sleigh bed, an antique cheval mirror, a rocking chair and a chest of drawers. The furniture almost filled the room, leaving scant space for the two adults to stand.

"I think this must have been a maid's room originally," Abbie said, inching away from Ben's imposing bulk. "But the windows make it light, and the heat from the kitchen rises to make it warm and cozy. I hadn't picked a room to sleep in, but now that Baby's here, I think this will do nicely."

Glaring at the minimal floor space, Ben harrumphed.

"Your approval overwhelms me." Abbie sat on the edge of the bed. When the baby seemed delighted with the motion, she bounced gently on the old springs. They creaked loudly, reminding her of the decrepit but noisy bed in Ben's college dormitory.

The look on Ben's face, astonishment followed rapidly by an undeniable sensuality, told her he remembered, too. "I'm going to check the rest of the house," he declared, his words brusque, his expression stormy. "Then I need to move on."

"Go right ahead. I'll stay here and feed Baby." She offered the child the bottle, glad for the distraction. Oh, how she needed a little breathing room.

Without looking up, she waved her free hand in the direction of a door to the left of the stairs. "That leads to the rest of the second story. There's a staircase to the attic. No basement. Only a crawl space accessible from the outside. There must be a flashlight somewhere around here, but I wouldn't know where—"

She caught herself babbling nervously, stopped and made the mistake of looking up.

He'd said he needed to head out, but he stood rooted to the spot, staring at her. No, not staring, devouring her with a smoldering regard. When she thought, at last, she would melt under his intensity, he turned and, without another word, left the room.

Mesmerized, she watched his broad back as he walked through the narrow doorway. My, what a large presence he created no matter where he went. He'd invaded her comfort zone, imprinting her new home with lingering traces of his strength and edgy masculinity. How was she ever going to cleanse the feel of him from her personal space?

Did she really want to?

As carefully as she'd tried to regulate her day-to-day existence, it seemed that life had a mischievous mind of its own. "Murphy," she muttered, "this better not be your doing, or you're fired as my guardian angel."

In response to her voice, the baby gurgled, blowing formula bubbles around the bottle's nipple. He seemed to think the whole situation funny.

What did babies know?

Chapter Four

Her heart and mind a jumble of emotions, Abbie gazed at the darkened window, now frosted with snow. It had been such a long time since she'd seen snow. How she'd missed it. The area of Texas where she and her parents had settled had never seen snow in the eight years they'd lived there.

The memory of Texas led her to a startling discovery. For an entire afternoon Abbie had not thought of herself as a breast cancer survivor. Instead, she'd been a woman caught up in a whirlwind of unconventional activity. Could this be good?

In the beginning, when her diagnosis had been new and raw and her treatment just started, doctors and fellow patients had warned her it was a mistake to try to forget she was sick. She must learn to integrate her illness into her daily life. But as the years accumulated, as her remission held, she allowed herself hope. Even then, she'd cautioned herself not to let go of the awareness that she'd been extraordinarily lucky, and had begun to wear her angel pin constantly as a reminder. Daily she walked a tightrope between preserving hope and facing reality, between optimism and truth-telling, between challenge and acceptance.

This afternoon she'd forgotten the tightrope.

The baby had fallen asleep while feeding. Abbie set the bottle on the floor, then turned the sleeping infant over her knees. She rubbed his back until she heard a drowsy burp. Carefully she laid him in the middle of her bed. She pulled out one of the chest drawers, then padded it with a folded blanket. Gently placing the sleeping baby in the drawer and covering him with the corner of a quilt, she went in search of Ben.

She needed to ask him one more important question before he left.

He was in the foyer downstairs. Obviously he'd come in from inspecting the crawl space. An aura of cold surrounded him. Cobwebs competed with snowflakes in his dark, tangled hair.

The out-of-doors and bracing weather had always been his element, had always made him look even more rugged, even more masculine, even more handsome than on an ordinarily drop-dead gorgeous day. Now, his eyes flashing, his color high, his hair whipped about his chiseled features, he seemed to have stepped out of a wilderness equipment catalog.

Abbie sucked in her breath.

The question she wanted to ask him just got harder to speak.

"The house seems structurally sound," he said, scowling.

"Don't sound so disappointed." She couldn't resist tweaking him and his edgy mood.

"I'm only thinking of the baby."

"Of course." She relaxed a little. His edginess actually created a distance she could live with. "But as I said before, the situation's only temporary. Janis promised to find a more permanent foster home by Monday."

"Yes." He appeared uncertain. "She may have something by tomorrow. Nine o'clock?"

"I'm sure Baby will have me up by then."

"I'm sure." He moved his lips in a half smile.

His softened expression made her bold. "Ben, I know my return to town has raised some eyebrows—"

"People will talk no matter what."

"I'm not worried about *people*. I'm concerned about the awkwardness between us. I want to explain what happened, but I need your full attention. Some time can we sit down alone together—"

"Not now." Without the baby between them, he seemed ready to bolt. "You heard me tell Janis I'm understaffed. I need to get back on duty."

"Before you go, let me ask this. Considering the baby and how he's thrown us together, do you see us becoming…you know…friends?"

He grew very still. The hungry look in his eyes that had so startled her in the bedroom returned. "I don't think so, Abbie."

"Oh."

She'd no sooner uttered the word, when he stepped

forward, sweeping her into his arms. He lowered his mouth to hers in a kiss that was as hot and ravenous as it was unexpected. He pulled her hard up against him and kissed her as if he were a man marooned and starving.

She smelled want in him, and her body responded in kind.

All those wonderful, sensual yearnings she'd kept at bay for years came crashing over her. Closing her eyes tightly to stem the flow of tears, she threaded her fingers through his damp hair and kissed him back, with a passion born of isolation and regrets.

He held her so tightly, she almost forgot to breathe.

When he swept his tongue across her lips, she opened for him. Tasted desire and the salt of the sea and home.

She ran her fingers down his temples, down his jaw rough with evening stubble, down his neck where the skin turned vulnerable.

He groaned and she absorbed the sound. She felt his breath, warm and ragged, on her cheek. Felt his hands possess her. Felt his strength envelop her.

This was the Ben she remembered. Only fiercer.

Suddenly he pulled away, but held her at arm's length with a forceful grip that bordered on painful. Passion and anger flickered in the depths of his heavy-lidded eyes. He reined in his emotions with obvious difficulty.

"Friends?" he repeated, pulverizing the word. "We'll never be friends as long as *that* stands between us."

She drew back, realizing he saw the kiss not as a homecoming, as she had, but as a warning.

He let her go and walked out of the cottage, leaving her feeling emotionally bruised and rejected.

What the hell had he done?

The bracing night air couldn't erase the feel of that disastrous kiss or of Abbie's reaction to it. He'd kissed her to warn her off and, in the process, to exorcise the traitorous physical attraction he still felt for her. But she hadn't accepted the warning. Instead, she'd kissed him back as if she were welcoming him home. And that damned physical ache that he'd tried to rid himself of? Its torment had only increased.

He couldn't forget her fingers in his hair, her body pressed to his. Her soft moan as she'd leaned into him. Her scent. Standing on her front step, Ben ran a gloved hand over his face in frustration. Even then he could still feel the sensation of his mouth on Abbie's.

Why had he acted the fool just now?

Because he'd been teed off at her offer of friendship.

He'd wanted to show her they couldn't be friends because that old unresolved sexual energy got in the way. Man, did it get in the way. Once you'd been Bogie and Bacall, you could never get back to Gilligan and Mary Ann.

Kissing Abbie to prove they'd moved irretrievably beyond friends, however, had been a big mistake. He'd lost his cool. And if there was one thing he'd learned the hard way, it was not to lose his cool. Never let 'em see you sweat. Never show your true emotions. Never let the other guy goad you into unthought-out action. Normally he was damn good at self-control. But in less than twenty-four hours back in town, Abbie Latham had pushed him to a place he hadn't visited with the worst of those who'd ridden the back of his cruiser in handcuffs.

She'd riled him. She'd pushed him over the edge. She'd driven him to outlandish behavior.

The kiss had been a foolhardy outward manifestation of an inward loss of cool. Period. And it had been incredibly stupid, leaving his motivation wide open for interpretation. He didn't need Abbie thinking he wanted a renewed relationship, because he didn't. Definitely not. How could you have a relationship with someone you couldn't rely on, couldn't trust to be open and honest? Couldn't trust to be there when the going got rough?

Right now he wished for an opportunity, any opportunity, to wash the taste of Abbie out of his mouth, to erase the feel of her from his arms, to prove in some irrevocable way—to himself, at least—that he was over her.

Angry, he stormed down the steps of the cottage and along the front path, only to pull up short at the sight of Serena's Volvo parked behind his cruiser. The Realtor sat in the police car's passenger seat.

Now what?

He opened the driver's door, then slid inside. "Hey, Serena. You waiting to see Abbie?"

"No." Cheeks flushed, Serena seemed agitated. "I was waiting for you."

"Trouble?"

"I don't know." She cut a quick glance at the cottage. "You tell me."

"Abbie found a baby—"

"I know about the baby."

"What, then?"

"Well...tongues were wagging today." She clasped and unclasped her hands. "I didn't realize you and Abbie Latham had such a history together."

"It's just that. History." He clutched the steering wheel. He didn't need to explain it to Serena, but apparently he should make it clear to himself. "She needed help with the baby. That's all."

Serena let out a long sigh. "Good. I thought I was too late."

"I don't understand." He had his suspicions, though.

"For the past few months I've waited quietly—patiently—thinking you might take the initiative. But when I learned how Abbie's return could complicate matters, I kicked myself for my forbearance."

"Meaning?"

"You silly, blind man. I would like *us* to have a relationship. There. I've said it."

"A relationship," he repeated. Hadn't he just now wished for something to take his mind off Abbie?

"Yes. More than an occasional coffee at the Wayside." Serena reached out and with a slender, gloved hand touched his thigh. "I thought maybe you could use a nightcap. At my place. Now. You've had an unusual day."

She didn't know how unusual.

"And Suki said you're technically off duty tonight."

Off duty, adult and single. What could be wrong with that?

"I've tried subtlety. It hasn't worked." Serena

trailed her fingers along his leg. "Now I'm asking you to come home with me."

How easy that would be. He bet he could erase the feel of Abbie's kiss in Serena's willing arms.

"I really like you, Ben."

And damned if he didn't like her. The thought struck him like a righteous bolt from the blue. Liking her, he wouldn't go home with her tonight because he'd end up leaving her, hurting their friendship. He wouldn't go home with her because passion might erase Abbie Latham, but *like* wouldn't. He'd end up with the torment that was Abbie, and Serena would end up with a bad attitude toward him. Or cops. Or men.

"Serena." He lifted her hand off his thigh. "You don't want to get involved with me. I don't have the best track record where relationships are concerned."

"You still love her." Serena's voice snagged on a note of desperation.

"No! It has nothing to do with her." He didn't speak her name in case the voicing of it proved him wrong. "I'm not comfortable with other people's needs. Deep down, emotional needs. Being a cop is tough enough with the community needs. I'm not looking for a personal relationship."

"Maybe relationship is too strong a word. I'd settle—"

"Don't settle, Serena." He briefly covered her mouth with his hand. "You deserve more."

"More…" Hurt in her eyes, she breathed the word with a shrug. "Why is it we always want a little bit more than we're ever going to get?"

He didn't know, but he hoped Abbie hadn't interpreted the kiss as the kind of longing Serena now displayed. Because that kiss wasn't longing. It was a warning there might still be something physical between them, but there was nothing—*nothing*—emotional. Or needy.

Physical was easy. Physical could act as an exorcism. Physical was what Serena would settle for if he'd only give the word. And why not say the word? He sure could use a dose of oblivion.

Serena stared at him, waiting. Trusting.

He couldn't abuse her trust.

"Can we be friends?" He winced at the false note those words struck, as false now as when Abbie had asked them of him earlier. Friendship was all he had to offer, though.

"I guess I don't have any choice." Serena hesitated in reaching for the door handle. "But I want you to know I don't consider this a closed discussion."

He didn't respond—he didn't want to encourage her, yet didn't want to insult or patronize her.

She leaned forward and planted a soft, lingering kiss on his mouth. An invitation. So different than the kiss with which he'd tried to warn Abbie off. "There's more where that came from."

When he'd kissed Abbie, he'd meant her to understand there would be absolutely no more where the first came from. But how had she received his message?

Slipping out of the car, Serena left Ben puzzling why her kiss couldn't mask the feel of Abbie's.

With mounting exasperation, he turned the key in the cruiser's ignition before he might feel compelled to take Serena up on her invitation.

Normally, he wasn't a man prone to temptation. Tonight, however, a vulnerability born of frustration dogged him mercilessly even though the proper path lay clear before him. Once he removed himself from the source of frustration—Abbie—he'd be fine. He needed to get through the weekend with her and the baby. Forty-eight hours. Then Janis would find a more permanent foster home. She had to. There weren't enough chocolate chip cookies in the world to bribe him into placing his heart in harm's way. In Abbie's way.

Because he was over her.

Hearing the cruiser start and pull away, Abbie wondered why Ben had sat so long in her front yard. She wished he'd come back in so they could thrash out the unspoken that lay thick and murky between them. Before she'd settled into Point Narrows she'd meant to make him understand her departure. But there had been Serena and then the baby and then Janis and then that kiss....

That kiss.

She crossed her hands over her chest and hugged herself to ward off the sudden chill coursing through her veins. In her decision to return home, she'd maintained an almost mantra-like belief she didn't want a renewal of a romantic relationship with Ben Chase. She'd made a decision eight years ago, and she would accept the consequences. She was alone now, and she was strong. But was it strength or protective coloration?

A part of her had avoided coming to terms with her present self as a whole and sexually attractive woman. In eight years she'd never tested those waters. Having met physical risks head-on, she preferred to defer the emotional risks.

"Oh, Murphy—" she sighed "—is my celibacy just another definition for cowardice?"

She needed to stop flying off into the land of *what if,* needed to dwell in the moment, to bring herself back to the task at hand. The baby.

Tiptoeing up the back stairs, she intended to check on him, then make herself some supper. But when she caught sight of the infant sleeping in his improvised crib, his sheer beauty made tears catch in her throat. She lay down upon the bed to watch him for just a moment.

Alone, Abbie allowed herself the luxury of savoring the baby's every movement. The flickering of his eyelids as he sank into deep sleep. The pursing of his full, pink lips as if he might find a little more supper. The flaring of his tiny nostrils as he breathed in precious life. All this she pressed to her memory in intimate detail.

This baby was as close to having children as she would ever come.

When Ben and Janis were around, Abbie grew painfully conscious of her very temporary caregiver's role. But alone, she could linger and pretend that the baby was her own. Forever. What harm could come of the fantasy as long as she kept it private?

From her position on the bed, she reached out and lightly lay her hand on the sleeping infant's chest.

"Sleep well," she whispered, overcome with maternal longing.

She pulled back, then closed her eyes to stem the rising flood of tears.

Mortified, Abbie stood alone in the kissing booth at the fair. Before she'd taken over the second shift, the waiting line had snaked out onto the midway. Men and boys had stood, dollar bills in hand, smiles on their faces in eager anticipation. But now that she stood ready to dispense the kisses, no one seemed interested. Ben walked by the booth twice without stopping. Her father, for pity's sake, kept his distance. When the fair organizer approached, checking on the needs of other booths, Abbie couldn't get him to make eye contact. Her girlfriends, whom she normally could count on for commiseration, shunned the area, too busy flirting with the boys, the boys who should be lined up—but weren't—at Abbie's booth.

Isolated, she stood listening to the pounding of her pulse in her ears. "I'm not a monster!" she whispered, sweat beginning to form at her hairline. "I'm still me!"

No one paid any heed.

She was like a tiny bead of oil in a vast ocean. A part but apart. And nothing she seemed to do integrated her with the vast, happy, milling current of humanity enjoying the fair.

Perhaps she wasn't alive. Perhaps she was a ghost. Invisible. To check, she pressed her trembling hands against the sharp edge of her stool until the pain made her wince. Ghosts didn't feel pain. "I'm alive!" she shouted.

The crowd grew uneasy.

She got off the stool. "And I'm not going away!"

She walked toward the nearest person, who skittered from her, leaving behind a trail of fear, as of cologne.

"I can't hurt you!" she cried, reaching out frantically as if in a child's game of blindman's bluff. "I'm not contagious!"

With each move she made, the crowd parted in revulsion, isolating her absolutely. Perspiration streamed down her temples, silent tears down her cheeks. Her heart thudded in her chest. What good was life if lived in rejection?

Desperate, she stumbled toward a retreating man. Ben...

Drenched in sweat and chilled through, Abbie sat bolt upright in bed. She reached for a light. Even in the lamp's soft glow, it took several minutes to identify the room. Not her bedroom in her parents' house in Texas, but a tiny back bedroom in Lily Arrondise's cottage. In Maine.

It took several more minutes for the terrifying dream to dissipate. For her pulse to return to normal.

Having fallen asleep watching the baby, Abbie still wore her skirt and sweater, both now damp and wrinkled. She checked on the tiny boy, who had begun to squirm with his eyes tightly shut. It wouldn't be long before he awoke, perhaps as damp as she and hungry. She needed to think beyond herself. She needed to shed her uncomfortable clothing and the dank feel of her dream.

As she rummaged through a suitcase for a flannel nightgown, she remembered how one of her dearest friends from therapy had confided that she'd suffered recurring nightmares of death. Not so Abbie.

She'd come face-to-face with death, had prepared

to embrace him, but at the last minute had backed away and made a bargain instead. She would entertain him by walking a tightrope—a thin emotional line on which she must balance between hope and reality, between optimism and truth-telling, between challenge and acceptance. Consequently, in coming to terms with her own mortality, she'd stepped through fear, clear out to the other side. And on the other side she'd discovered a heightened awareness of being present in life.

She'd been blessed. With every checkup for the past seven years her body had been cancer free. She and her parents celebrated each new day of life as if it were their last.

Courage had begun to keep company with self-doubt. She began to live with an intense appreciation of the preciousness of life, and, without turning her back on reality, she made a conscious effort to make hope her lifelong partner.

No, she didn't fear death, which was an inescapable part of life. She feared rejection, had felt rejection in varying degrees when she'd been honest about her cancer with those who were cancer free. Yet no one could convince her rejection was an inevitable part of life. She would work to turn rejection into understanding and acceptance. Carefully. Thoughtfully. One day at a time.

She'd begin with Ben Chase.

Finding her favorite soft and worn nightgown, she stripped off her sweater, then her skirt, stockings and shoes. Swinging around to face herself in the old cheval mirror, she took a deep breath.

After many years she'd come to terms with who

she had become as a result of her battle with cancer, but every time she saw herself naked in a mirror, she saw herself as a cancer-free person might see her.

As a man might see her.

As Ben might see her.

Slowly, deliberately, she removed her bra with the prosthesis in the left cup. Tenderly she raised her right hand and placed it along the faintly silver scar that ran from her armpit diagonally across her chest.

Her badge of courage. That's what she called it.

But would a cancer-free person see it that way?

Would a love interest?

Would Ben, if given the opportunity?

Would he understand why she hadn't chosen reconstructive surgery?

Many of her fellow breast cancer survivors hadn't understood, for this was a hot button issue with no easy answers.

In Abbie's mind, reconstruction would not bring back her breast, her real breast. But more importantly, she wanted *nothing* standing in the way of future early detection. Other's might decide differently, but she had made her decision and had never looked back.

Would Ben understand?

The baby's cry pierced the night.

"There, there," she cooed, thrusting her nightgown over her head, then moving to pick up the little boy. "Let's get you changed and fed. I know exactly what wet and hungry feels like."

As she held the baby to her, he nuzzled her chest, rooting around for a breast, for milk, for comfort.

"You're out of luck, Bucko," she murmured,

stroking his downy head, not quite knowing whether to laugh or cry.

In the kitchen she quickly changed the fretting infant while a bottle of formula heated in a saucepan on the stove. The little boy, sensing a meal just out of reach, increased the level of his howls.

"Babyface," she crooned, "you must learn a little patience. Otherwise all is suffering."

The child stopped crying for a second, cocked one eyebrow as if to say, "Let's cut the metaphysical bullroar," then jump-started a roar of his own.

Not having a free wrist on which to test the heated formula, Abbie held the bottle above her face and squirted a stream into her mouth. "Eeeuuuw! If you're smart, you'll grow up quickly and graduate to something palatable."

When she rubbed the bottle's nipple against the baby's lower lip, he seized his supper as if it were ambrosia.

"So much for your sophisticated taste buds." Abbie chuckled as she settled herself in a rocker by the stove.

She glanced at her watch. Four o'clock. You couldn't tell it by the snow-crusted windows, however. Sometime during the night the polar express had pulled into Point Narrows and now seemed determined not to leave the station.

There were those who reacted to the long Maine nights with an irritable claustrophobia. Not Abbie. Accustomed to a metaphysical darkness crouching at the edges of her existence, she chose to focus on the light.

It was light in her kitchen. And warm. And cozy.

A light danced in the baby's eyes now that he had his meal. He didn't care that the woman holding him had one breast.

Abbie's heart melted.

Life was good.

She needed to explain the goodness to Ben. As much as she feared rejection, she needed to make him understand her leaving him eight years ago wasn't a repudiation but a gift. A misguided gift, perhaps, but a gift all the same.

"What do you think?" she asked the baby. "I bet your mommy thought she was doing the right thing by you. I bet she'd been watching the library. Bet she saw how many people came and went. Thought that someone would find you and take better care of you than she can right now. For whatever reasons."

Batting his thick fringe of eyelashes, the baby grunted with contentment.

"She's coming back. I can feel it." Abbie rocked, letting the rhythm soothe them both. "Then it'll be her job to explain and our job to understand."

The baby waved a chubby hand before slapping it back on his bottle.

"She loves you, you know. Your mommy." Abbie brushed her lips over the soft skin of the child's forehead. "There are so many ways to show love, some more hurtful than others. If we're lucky, we get a second chance to try to make up for the pain."

Chapter Five

Eight inches of snow had fallen overnight. Eight inches of snow had kept Ben from getting to Abbie's before Janis so he could effect some damage control. If kissing Abbie to gain some distance had been a bad plan, he needed a new one. The new one involved an apology for his behavior last night, then some straight talk. He didn't need Janis as an audience. He'd planned to get to Abbie's early, but the first significant snowfall of the year had caused traffic mishaps that had involved his professional attention and delayed his arrival at the Arrondise cottage.

"Don't you love a Christmas snow?" Janis chirped as she and Ben stood on Abbie's front step, waiting for a response to their knock.

No, he couldn't say as he did. "Nice," he muttered, trying not to appear a total Scrooge.

"Is there something you're not telling me, Ben Chase?" Janis could always sense the unsaid.

Abbie, baby cradled on her shoulder, opened the door, saving him an explanation. "Come out of the cold!" she exclaimed, ducking behind the door. "Don't worry about the snow or your boots. I haven't had time to shovel the walk."

She gently jiggled the wide-awake child in her arms. The child, in fact, looked far more awake than Abbie. Her otherworldly beauty was marred by dark circles under her eyes. "Baby's kept me busy this morning."

"You look exhausted." Concerned, Ben scowled at her as he stood aside for Janis to enter the house first. How much strength did she have after her unspecified illness?

Janis shot Ben a perplexed glance. "I like to start with 'good morning' myself." She held up a bakery box. "Sticky buns, as promised."

"Yum!" Abbie closed the door behind her guests. "I'll have to get out later to work off the extra calories."

"You're not planning on driving, are you?" Ben couldn't shake his irritation. He didn't know how Abbie had interpreted last night's kiss, and, until he did, he was uneasy about her expectations. His uneasiness made him surly. "There are eight new inches of snow out there. Slippery snow."

"Good! I found an old sled in the breezeway off the kitchen and thought if the sun came out and the wind died down, I could strap the car seat to the sled and take Baby for a spin around the block." She cocked one eyebrow, challenging. "Unless I'm under house arrest with this assignment."

"Not that I'd heard of." Janis shot a frown at Ben. "I took every one of my children for daily walks, no matter the weather, and they've all grown up to be healthy as harbor seals."

"Well, that settles that." Abbie smiled sweetly at Ben. "Coffee?"

"No. Thanks." He pinched the bridge of his nose to keep from looking at her soft lips, thinking of that ill-advised kiss. "I'll clear your walk. I have a shovel in the cruiser."

Janis put out a hand to detain him. "Please, stay. I think the three of us need to talk. This foster situation is a team effort."

He knew they'd agreed to cooperate, but that didn't mean he had to be comfortable with the decision. Pushing aside his discomfort, he stayed. For the baby.

Abbie looked pleased. Tired, but pleased. Did she want him here? "Three coffees it is." She nuzzled the baby and looked every inch a mother. "Formula for you, my sweet."

Ben had enjoyed holding the baby yesterday, even though the act had triggered old, long-forgotten yearnings. The memory of his vulnerability made him even more irritable.

"Let me hold him." Handing Ben the box of sticky buns, Janis quickly shrugged out of her coat. "He's beautiful. And seems so content."

"Now, yes. But he had a fussy morning. *Early* morning. Nothing seemed to comfort him for long." Abbie exchanged baby for coat, then hung the coat in a hall closet. She turned to the kitchen. "I admit I ran through my repertoire of kiddie entertainment."

"I told you to call me if you ran into trouble." Ben hadn't wanted her to call him, but now that she hadn't, he felt exasperation at her independent attitude. She looked worn-out, but still she hadn't called in the reserves. Stubborn woman.

Stubborn, inscrutable woman. What did she want from him? Did she want anything? Why did he care?

He loosened his jacket, but kept it on as he followed Abbie and Janis into the kitchen. He wasn't staying long if he couldn't shake Janis or this tenacious bad mood.

"No trouble," Abbie insisted, taking charge in the old-fashioned kitchen, pouring coffee into Lily Arrondise's bone china cups. "I think Baby simply missed his mother."

"That's understandable," Janis cooed. "Everyone needs his mother."

That did it for Ben. Exasperation boiled over. He thumped the sticky-bun box down on the table. "Why do you two think this child is better off with a woman who dumped him on the doorstep of a public building?"

Her eyes large, Abbie paused, the coffeepot hovering over one delicate cup. "We don't know the circumstances of the mother's disappearance. She may have made the wrong choice for all the right reasons."

"She may be in trouble," Janis chimed in.

"She might be broke, alone, frightened or unwell." Her gaze on Ben steady and probing, Abbie set the coffeepot down on the kitchen table. "Leaving Baby as she did might be her cry for help. We need to find her. Help her.''

''We need to find her and bring her to justice.'' Ben simmered, but kept his voice in check so as not to frighten the baby.

There had been no justice when Sandra Chase had abandoned her family. Maybe with this unwanted child, he could create some balance in the universe. The knot tightened in the pit of his stomach. ''Abbie, we've gone over this.''

Janis cut him a surprised look.

''And we didn't come to a consensus, did we?'' Abbie jutted out her chin, as determined as she'd been in high school and college when she'd seized a cause. ''We need to work together on this.''

''No. You need to take care of the baby. I need to find the mother. They're two separate issues. No consensus needed.''

The baby whimpered.

''What is going on here?'' Janis asked in a hushed voice, rocking the child close, a hand over his exposed ear. ''You vouched for Abbie, Ben. I thought the two of you were friends. You sound like rivals bickering on the playground.''

Provoked, Ben ran his hand through his hair. ''We see the world differently,'' he replied, leaving the friends issue untouched.

''Oh, is that it?'' Janis didn't look as if she believed his story for a minute, but she let it drop.

''Please, sit,'' Abbie urged, placing the sticky buns on a platter alongside the coffee cups.

The three adults sat warily around the table. Ben had created a discordant atmosphere with his outburst earlier. He reminded himself of his personal buzz phrase, *self-control*. But self-control was difficult when everything in his morning seemed outside his comfort zone and beyond his control.

He sat across the table from the woman who was supposed to have been his wife, next to a baby he could imagine as their son. He couldn't get his fingers through the tiny china handles of the coffee cup, although he desperately needed a stiff jolt of caffeine. His body temperature ran alternately hot and cold in a house where the heating system needed treatment for schizophrenia. And the overly cluttered kitchen made him feel like an outsize oddity, an outsider clueless as to what was expected of him emotionally.

The two women stared at him without flinching.

"What steps have you taken to find the mother?" Janis asked at last.

"The investigation." He exhaled, surprised to find he'd been holding his breath, relieved to be asked to talk about the search, a matter of facts, bits of manageable information, not the slippery slope of emotions surrounding his relationship with Abbie. "We took prints off the basket. I've contacted the area high schools to get the names of girls formerly in the program for pregnant teens. The local hospital to see if, in the past several months, anyone gave birth whom the staff might have considered at risk maternally. And police throughout the state for an update on runaways. It's a start."

"A good one." Janis always proved quick with a positive stroke.

"How about you?" he asked. "Any luck coming up with a less temporary foster home?"

When she made a show of adjusting the baby's sleeper, Ben knew the news wouldn't be positive.

"It doesn't matter," Abbie said quickly. "There's no reason I can't take him indefinitely."

"You have a job." He failed to smother the argumentative demon within him.

"I have a quiet job in a library." That old feisty glint showed in Abbie's eyes. "Baby doesn't even roll over yet. He'll be fine in his car seat on the checkout desk."

"Catching germs from every schoolkid who signs out a book." Ben shook his head at her naiveté.

"You were the one who suggested Margot take Baby. She works. At a cash register, no less. I suppose money is germ free—"

"Pipe down, you two," Janis cautioned. "Time out, in fact." She shot them a look of exasperation. "I'll feed the baby while you take a walk and resolve whatever's really bothering you. When you've declared a truce, come back inside, so we can focus on the welfare of this child."

"Not necessary." The last thing Ben wanted was the first thing he'd wanted. Time alone with Abbie. But where he'd initially anticipated the baby as a buffer, Janis now suggested a head-to-head. Dangerous territory. "We're cool."

"I think a walk is just what we need." Casting a pointed look in Ben's direction, Abbie stood. "We have a few details from last night to iron out."

Last night.

The two words stuck him like a cattle prod, rendering him both electrified and speechless. He stood as Abbie went to the hall closet to get her coat.

"This contrariness isn't like you, Ben," Janis said quietly, looking up from settling the baby with his bottle. Her gaze held compassion as well as question.

"It's the season. The department's a zoo."

"Then a brisk walk should do you good. Stretch those tense muscles. Clear the cobwebs." She smiled as Abbie reentered the room. "Take your time."

Why not? Abbie had taken eight years to explain her behavior. He suspected she still hadn't come fully clean. The thought didn't put him in a communicative frame of mind.

Self-control, he reminded himself. *Self-control.*

Abbie noted Ben's stony features, his unyielding posture. Was that fear in the pit of her stomach at the thought of being alone with him?

No, not fear. Anxiety, surely. Anticipation, perhaps. But not fear. Fear was what she'd felt when the doctor had handed down her breast cancer diagnosis. Shock and fear had made her run so as not to spread that desperation to the one she'd loved above all others.

In running, she may have lost Ben's love, but in coming back, she wanted to regain his respect. To do that, she must carefully unfold her story in words he could understand without pity or loathing.

Last night's kiss—and the anger behind it—was a symptom of his lack of understanding.

"Are you ready?" she asked. Was *she?* Now, there was the million-dollar question.

He buttoned his coat in silent answer.

She led the way outside, into the clean, crisp morning-after. Barely off the front steps, Ben stopped.

"About last night," he said. "About the kiss. I'm sorry. It was a stupid thing to do."

"But you wanted to make it clear—"

"*Very* clear."

"That we—"

"Yes."

She almost smiled. "That we *what,* Ben?"

"That we're history."

"So you kissed me."

"Yeah." He shook his head as if he couldn't believe it himself. "To prove it was physical. Nothing more." A pained expression crossed his face. "Maybe that's all it ever was between us. Physical attraction."

"It was more." Oh, it was much, much more.

"Then why did you leave? Tell me."

She took a deep breath of the pungent marine air. "I'm ready to start."

"Start? Don't play games with me, Abbie. I don't have the time or the inclination."

"Do you remember my aunt Sophie?"

"Yeah. The one who died of Alzheimer's when we were in high school."

"And do you remember how Uncle Marcus suffered right along with her? How he died shortly after Aunt Sophie? Of a broken heart, my parents said."

"What do they have to do with us?" Ben moved from foot to foot in the heavy snow, his motion making a crunching that underscored his restlessness.

She tried not to hurry. She'd come so far and learned so much, but it had taken her eight years. She feared overwhelming Ben by telescoping her journey. "Remember we talked about how we didn't know if we could handle a situation like that, how badly it would hurt.''

A slow realization crossed Ben's face. ''How sick were you?''

She'd wanted to prepare him somehow. But perhaps it was better to get the explanation over quickly. She wouldn't say painlessly.

''I thought I was going to die.'' She paused as deep shadows of incredulity flickered in his eyes.

''And you wanted to die alone?''

''I wanted to spare you the pain my uncle went through.''

''Ah, Abbie, you never really knew me, did you?'' He passed his hand over his eyes. ''Twice in my career I thought I might die. Both times I wasn't afraid of death, but of dying alone. Without my loved ones around me. I wouldn't have shut them out. I needed them. Imagined them needing me if the shoe were on the other foot. That need kept me going.''

He looked away, between the houses across the street where the harbor sparkled in the pale winter sunlight, the incoming tide swelling the marshes and inlets. ''But what does that prove? You and I have always been opposites.''

His tightly checked anger mirrored the anger she'd felt when she'd first heard her diagnosis. As much as it hurt her to watch his reaction, she needed to allow him his journey.

He swallowed hard. ''I could have helped you. Loved you. No matter the outcome. But you booted me from your life.''

''I was selfish, too. I couldn't bear the thought of your pity. Or your revulsion.''

"Good God, Abbie, what kind of disease are we talking about?"

"Cancer." There, she'd said it, an ugly word at first saying, but a word she'd incorporated into who she was.

Ben flinched. It wasn't an easy word to absorb. "Cancer." He repeated the word between clenched teeth as if he could crush it. His jaw went rigid, his eyes glistened. "Not you, Abbie. Not you."

"Yes, me." Her hand fluttered to Murphy on her lapel.

His face had become a mask to his emotions. He seemed to slip away from her. What was he feeling? Bitterness? Pity? Revulsion?

She needed to hang on to him with words if nothing else. "At my last checkup," she continued, "when my oncologist told me my remission held, I told myself I needed to move beyond survival. I needed to *live*. I decided to come home then. To Point Narrows."

It had been easier telling her decision to her parents than to Ben. To her parents her return to Maine had meant a heart-wrenching separation. They wouldn't return with her. Point Narrows had been her diagnosis. Their despair. Texas was hope. A new life. They wept over her decision.

But to Ben her return must seem like a slap in the face. He'd recoiled as if it had been.

"Talk to me." She strove not to lose him. "I won't break."

Anger returned to his features. "I'm sorry for what you've been through. I can't imagine the battle." He looked her right in the eyes. "That's what sticks in my throat, you see. I can't imagine because I wasn't there. You didn't think I was strong enough to handle it.''

''No! You're one of the strongest people I know.''

''Then what?''

''I let you go so that you could move on in case…the worst happened.''

''But it didn't.''

''No, it didn't. I was lucky.''

''And I was unlucky.''

She had no answer to that. ''I'm sorry I hurt you.'' Words couldn't convey the depths of her regret, and she fought back the tears that might.

The frosty Maine air seeped into her coat. She turned her collar up for protection, but no amount of worsted wool could protect her from Ben's icy glare. His silence chilled her more than the gusts of wind off the harbor.

Her oncologist had warned her that people would react to news of her illness in a myriad of ways.

But Ben wasn't just *people*.

She'd meant to begin her story to open up communication with him, to foster understanding, to gain, if nothing else, a sense of closure for both of them. But here he stood, only several feet away physically, but how many miles emotionally? With his sustained silence, she saw him retreating to that internal fortress from which he'd always guarded his true feelings. He needed to hear more. Much more. If he pulled up the drawbridge, however, she wouldn't get her chance to tell him. Time might help. But she'd come to view time as fickle. Untrustworthy as an ally.

Without speaking, he walked to the police cruiser

parked in her drive. At first she thought he was leaving. But he opened the trunk, then withdrew a shovel and a bag of road salt. Silently he brushed by her, dropped the bag on the first step and began shoveling her walk with a vengeance. She had to step backward to keep out of the way of shovel and flying snow.

"Ben. Did you hear me? I'm sorry. Truly sorry. Can you understand why—"

"I heard you." He never stopped shoveling. Perspiration began to glisten on his forehead. "But I don't understand. I don't understand why you left, and I sure as hell don't understand why you came back."

She'd expected to lose him at first, but the reality hurt more than the visualization.

"I left," she began cautiously, "so as not to infect you with the desperation I felt. I came back to pull my life into balance."

He thunked the shovel on the cleared pavement, leaned on the handle, glared at her. "Balance. What does that mean, Abbie?"

Oh, dear. How difficult it was to think under his unrelenting blue gaze. She swallowed hard and felt the meaning of balance elude her.

"I wanted to come back where I felt safe," she ventured. "To a job I always wanted. To live each day with joy. With friends."

His look said the kiss last night had squelched the friends issue, at least between the two of them. But he said nothing, turning instead to shovel the drive in long steady scoops toward the street. His movements were spare, his attitude stoically aloof. He'd dismissed her.

How she wanted to reach out to him as she had in years gone by. She knew from experience his silence covered pain. She wanted to massage the taut muscles at the back of his neck, brush the hair away from his temples, tell him with her touch that things would work out. As she'd told him years ago. But she was younger then, and more naive. She knew now that when things did work, the working out was often not the way you expected.

Ben hadn't expected her explanation.

Filled with empathy, she wanted to kiss the fan of lines etched at the corners of his eyes, then drew back, startled, at the physicality of her desire.

They'd been talking about sacrifice and balance only seconds before. Where had this unsubtle and unsuitable yearning come from?

Watching him shovel. Watching him move. Watching him withhold. Watching him mesmerized her. Always had. His brand of masculinity made it impossible not to watch, impossible not to want, not to think of the possibilities.

How had she convinced herself she was over Ben Chase?

The truth slapped her. For eight years, although she'd sublimated the thought of him in the name of survival, she'd never given him up. Her holding on made her return to Point Narrows a lie. She hadn't returned for balance. Her balance had been an artificial construct. She'd returned with the gambler's hope for reconciliation. With Ben.

My, but that bit of truth struck as a bolt from the blue.

The wind kicked up. A seagull shrieked overhead.

Clouds played tag with the sun. Scrunching her collar more tightly about her throat, Abbie felt the scratch of her little guardian angel pin on her cheek. "Murphy, what are you trying to tell me?" she muttered.

Murphy was always telling her to seize the day.

"It's not that easy," she whispered. Seizing and balancing were far too often in opposition.

From the end of the driveway, Ben raised his head and shot her a glance as if he'd caught her talking to herself. Conversing with Murphy sometimes proved risky business.

A long time ago an oncology nurse had suggested Abbie "let it all out" by talking to an inanimate object—a kind of scream-therapy-meets-its-mantra. Abbie had tried it on Murphy and had found it therapeutic. Not long afterward Murphy started talking back.

All in all, the little gilt talisman was easier to communicate with than Ben Chase.

Ben began to widen the clearing back up the drive from the road. Abbie could tell nothing from the set of his face, from his hooded eyes or the mechanical swing of his body. For all she knew he could be thinking about traffic reports. Only the way he refused to look at her told her he was working her words, setting them into his universe.

Yes, she wanted to comfort him. Wanted him.

What a fraud she'd turned out. She desired him, but knew she wouldn't act on her desire. After eight years of cultivating a cautious, moment-by-moment way of life, she couldn't, wouldn't, seize the day and take the steps necessary to effect more than a simple truce with Ben Chase. Despite her yearning, she couldn't chance projecting him in the role of renewed flame because she'd told him only part of her story. The untold parts loomed as daunting hurdles. Her mastectomy, for starters.

Whether she'd truly come back to Point Narrows for emotional balance was a moot issue. She *needed* balance. Contemplating a relationship revival with Ben rocked her very existence, like a dory on a storm-tossed sea.

But, oh, how she wanted Ben Chase.

Coming to the end of the drive, Ben paused with his back to Abbie and looked out at the woods behind the Arrondise cottage. He could feel Abbie's gaze upon him and felt churlish in his silence.

Cancer.

His Abbie had cancer.

It had taken courage to tell that story. She'd told it with shoulders straight, with gaze unwavering, had shared a darkness terrifying to contemplate. Now she expected a reaction. She'd always encouraged him to share his feelings, something he found next to impossible. Now she deserved a reaction.

But how could he react without appearing small?

His first reaction had been to take her in his arms, to shield her from the specter of death. The thought of losing her twisted his gut in knots. But she'd thwarted death alone, and he'd lost her anyway.

It was his anger that made him feel small.

How did you deal with a rival like cancer? It wasn't like another man. Wasn't like a change of heart. Not like love gone stale. Those were challenges he could meet head-on. But cancer. A life-threatening disease. If he saw cancer as a rival, he was a chump. Petty.

He'd always believed he could protect her, had looked forward to speaking his marriage vows, to making public his deep and abiding love. But she hadn't let him speak or protect. And for that he was angry.

Angry at a woman who'd gone through hell.

What kind of reaction was that? What kind of a man did that make him?

As hard as he tried, he could not begin to unknot the pain at his core.

"I'd better get in." Her voice drifted over his shoulder. "Janis must have papers for me to sign."

Don't go. Although the words blared in his head, he couldn't utter them. He turned around to look at her. *There's so much left unsaid.* Her pain. His pain.

It would take only a step to execute his first reaction, to take her in his arms—

"Why, Ben Chase and Abbie Latham!" Clucky Tillman, the town's worst gossip, slid her Jeep to a halt at the end of the drive. "Fancy seeing you two together again! And that must be Janis McDougal's car. The baby! How's that poor little baby?"

"The baby's fine, Ms. Tillman." Abbie stood erect, her collar pulled tightly against the bracing air. She looked strong and vulnerable at the same time.

Ben took a step closer to her. The anger he'd felt earlier dissolved to an edgy emotional shield in the face of Clucky's nosiness.

"How's Serena taking all this?" Clucky smirked as she skewered Ben with a beady stare.

"The rental?" Deliberately misunderstanding the question, Ben turned to indicate the Arrondise cottage. "Why, I suspect she's real pleased, seeing it's hard to find tenants outside the summer season."

Abbie's expression seemed to twinkle inside her raised collar.

Clucky huffed, obviously put out that she hadn't gotten a rise out of him. "Janis taking the baby away?"

"No, ma'am." Abbie stepped closer to Ben. "I'm fostering him until a less temporary home can be found."

"A young woman like you!" Clucky rolled her eyes dramatically. "You don't need to be wasting your time with foster kids. Get a man. Raise a family of your own."

Abbie dropped her collar. Her face went dead white except for a red scratch the gold pin had made on her cheek. Her eyes showed a pain she hadn't revealed when she'd talked about her illness. Her posture sagged. She turned and, without another word, walked into the cottage.

"Touchy, that girl," Clucky said, remorseless. "Must be the snooty Latham blood." She put the Jeep in gear and sped away, leaving Ben furious, more furious with Clucky for the obvious pain she'd caused Abbie than he had been with Abbie for the pain she'd caused him.

He supposed he should be grateful to the old Tillman bat. She'd created a perfect opportunity for him to leave. But an ancient protectiveness rose to the fore, and he started for the house in search of Abbie.

"Ben!" A car had pulled into the drive and three women, headed by Meg Nichelini, tumbled out, laden with bags and baby accoutrements. Meg was wife to his best friend, Dante, and one of the most generous women he knew.

"News travels fast." If any more people showed up, he wouldn't have to shovel the drive. It would be trampled bare.

The other women smiled and nodded as they trooped up the front steps, but Meg stopped. "We haven't seen much of you lately."

"Been busy."

"It's good you're helping out with this baby." Her voice was noncommittal, but her expression said she'd like to hear the whole story if he had time.

He didn't. "I'm just one of many." He nodded after the two women Janis had just let into the house. "Looks like the little guy's welfare is a community endeavor."

"'Tis the season." Meg turned to follow the other women. "Coming in?"

"No." Whatever had made Abbie bolt earlier, she'd be okay, surrounded by Meg and her crew of wise women. She didn't need him. Shouldn't need him. "Tell Janis she knows where to find me."

"And Abbie?"

"Just tell her goodbye."

Chapter Six

Meg Nichelini's team of women entered Abbie's life like an invigorating seasonal change. Having raided the church thrift shop, they brought gently used baby clothes, extra supplies, a portable crib and a bustling diversion to the hurt Abbie had experienced with Clucky's thoughtless remark and the unaccountable regret she'd felt when Ben had not reappeared.

Abbie knew Meg from hearsay. Four years older, Meg had left Point Narrows as Abbie entered high school. Meg had been pregnant. Although she'd decided to keep the baby the father had decided he wouldn't marry her. The rumors and innuendo that had trailed Meg then were as thick as those that swirled around Abbie now. Abbie wondered how Meg had handled her initial return to town. Obviously she'd coped with aplomb, because here she headed up a group of women as if she were a born community leader, relaxed with those who might or might not have delighted in passing around her story. Abbie could learn much from Meg Nichelini.

Aside from rumors, Abbie grappled with the concept of relaxed female camaraderie. Ben, school studies and her parents' social obligations had made up her earlier life in Point Narrows, leaving little time for lighthearted acquaintances. Later, her concerted effort at survival in Texas colored each new relationship with an intensity that eclipsed casual.

Now, surprisingly, Baby, a boy in uneasy circumstances, had introduced an estrogen easiness to her new home. Laughter. Gentle kidding. A morning of decidedly female cooperation for which she gave thanks.

She stood with Meg at the kitchen sink, washing up the cups and saucers, the pastry plates. Having bathed, fed, changed and played with Baby, the two women who'd accompanied Meg had walked home, insisting they needed the exercise after Janis's sticky buns. Meg and Janis lingered.

At the table Janis gathered up the necessary signed papers. "Well, that does it. Don't hesitate to call if you need anything." She placed a magnetized business card on the refrigerator. "Because Ben's checking in, I'm not going to worry. You'll be fine."

"I don't know that Ben will be checking in." Frowning, Abbie pulled the plug from the sink drain. "He told Meg to tell me goodbye."

"Oh, I don't think he meant it in any permanent way," Meg replied.

Janis paused in organizing her briefcase. "Did you

straighten out your differences?'' She etched her question with motherly concern.

''We tried.'' Abbie wiped her hands on a towel. ''Ben and I have a ways to go.''

Perplexed, Meg glanced from one woman to the next, but remained silent.

''I'll talk to him before I return to the office,'' Janis declared.

''No. I'll talk to him.'' Abbie took a deep breath. ''Ben is…stressed. I know how dangerous it is to allow stressful emotions to fester. I'm going to keep at him until we've cleared the air. It's ancient history that lies between the two of us. Just the two of us. We don't need to pull anyone else into the tension. We'll get through it.''

''Or go nuts trying.'' Meg rolled her eyes. ''I know Ben Chase. As stubborn as my Dante. You have your job cut out for you.''

''I don't have time for stubborn.''

''Baby,'' Janet cautioned, slipping into her coat, ''Baby is your top priority, Abbie.''

Smiling, Abbie showed Janis to the door. ''You can rest assured Baby is job number one around here.''

In her heart she wondered at the response she'd get if her parents or her oncologist ever heard such a statement from her. They'd made her promise *she* would be job number one. Feeling as if she'd sneaked out of line and out on a limb, she marveled at how the risk intoxicated rather than frightened her.

''Good girl.'' Janis patted Abbie on the shoulder. ''Catch you later. Goodbye, Meg!'' she called into the kitchen. ''Your halo's in the mail!''

Shutting the door behind Janis, Abbie turned to find

Meg gathering her things. "Can you stay?" Of all the women, Abbie felt drawn to the plainspoken Meg.

Meg was forthright, yes, but she didn't dig for information that wasn't offered. Perhaps she'd suffered from too much nosy excavation into her own behavior. Perhaps she'd developed compassion from the scrutiny. In any event, although she'd seemed perplexed by Abbie and Janis's exchange, Meg didn't press the issue further.

"I can stay for a few minutes." She glanced at her watch. "I have to make sure I'm out of here to take my daughter to a birthday party. Her first. She's three." She cocked her head and waited. "What's on your mind?"

"I know Janis is supposed to be my contact, but she's so busy. And Ben's supposed to be my backup, but—"

"You and he have locked horns."

"To put it mildly." Abbie sighed. "I'd feel more comfortable if I could call you for baby advice."

"Be my guest." With a pen Meg scribbled her number on a paper napkin. "But I can't imagine you having any trouble. You're a natural."

Abbie blushed.

"Did I say something wrong?"

"No. It's just that I can't have children." Now, why had she revealed that fact to an almost complete stranger?

"I'm sorry." The simplicity of Meg's response, the warmth, not pity, in her eyes answered Abbie's unspoken question. "Be careful with Baby," Meg added gently. "One day you'll have to let him go."

"Oh, I'm very good at letting go." However, the

thought of the beautiful little boy flooded Abbie with an emotional vulnerability. "But I don't see Baby as just a weekend responsibility. I see him as a symbol of a new beginning, of a chance to connect to the future."

"A precious connection his missing mother has broken."

Meg's words startled Abbie. Hadn't she broken just such a precious connection with Ben? Could she find a way to reconnect? Even if they could work through their present communications difficulties, would Ben consider a renewed relationship if he knew she lived, of necessity, moment to moment, if he knew she would never have children of her own?

Abbie shook off her wayward thoughts. "Well, this morning Baby had five mothers. Fairy godmothers you were!" she exclaimed, hugging Meg impulsively.

Meg laughed. "Let's hope the wicked fairy doesn't show up as in all the old tales."

"Don't worry. That's over and done. Clucky Tillman came and went before you arrived."

"Ah, every age has its troublemaker. When I returned to Point Narrows five years ago, I offended Lettie Moore's sense of morality. She was postmistress at the time. Neither rain nor sleet not dark of night could lessen her interest in my business."

"You?"

"It's a long story. We'll have to do lunch one day, and I'll tell it. There's a new diner up on Route One with a list of chocolate desserts that'll make your toes curl." She slipped on her jacket. "Until then, a little advice from Meg. Nothing makes a busybody hotter than being ignored."

"That's so true. And so easily forgotten." Abbie followed Meg to the door. "I've been dealing with some pretty heavy issues and managing quite well. I don't know why I let the small stuff bother me."

"It's always the small stuff that trips us up." Meg bussed Abbie on the cheek. "Welcome home. I have a feeling we're going to be good friends."

"I feel in need of a friend." Abbie smiled and felt a warm satisfaction descend upon her. "You see, I'm on the brink of a new adventure."

As Meg opened the door, Baby set up a wail from his crib upstairs. "Adventure calls," Meg declared. "I'll let myself out."

With a lighter heart than she'd felt in ages, Abbie made her way to tend to the small stuff with the very large set of lungs. It amazed her how babies got what they wanted. Tenacity and a grand sense of the moment. Perhaps she could take a lesson.

From a central vantage point beside the lobster-trap Christmas "tree," Ben watched holiday merrymakers fill Point Narrows' square for the town's annual Prelude festivities. Intermittent clouds scudded across the afternoon sun, but the weather held mostly clear and crisp and Christmassy. The town's half-dozen or so specialty shops and galleries were open and doing a booming business, all to the accompaniment of bell ringers standing before the library. Herbie Thurow sold more evergreen trees and wreaths and hot chocolate outside M & M Hardware than he did gas. Ben's brother Garrett gave hayrides to the community pier on his flatbed truck, which usually served to haul traps. People trooped in and out of the church parlor for the Holly Tea as they kept watch on the harbor. At three o'clock Santa was due to appear on a lobster boat to dispense candy to the kids.

As police chief, Ben was an old hand at Christmas Prelude. Although he circulated, he couldn't really say he kept the peace. Year after year, the crowds were manageable, the event predictable. Except for this year. Abbie's return had thrown predictability into a cocked hat.

The appearance of one tiny baby and Janis's insistence that Ben help Abbie with the child had further pushed prediction into no-man's-land.

The last straw, the unwelcome attraction he still felt for Abbie, had shocked him, had made him edgy and on guard. He couldn't predict his emotional reactions from one minute to the next. He had trouble enough getting through the Christmas season without Abbie poking at the chink in his armor.

"Hi." The soft, all-too-familiar voice at his elbow made him start. Abbie.

He jerked around to find her coming upon him from behind, pulling an old sled with a car seat strapped to it. Bundled almost beyond recognition, the baby slept serenely in his oddly rigged winter stroller.

"Hi." He tried to sound noncommittal, disinterested, but the image of her running from Clucky's comment earlier softened his heart against his will. "Are you okay?"

"Me?" She appeared startled by his question. "I'm fine."

"You didn't seem so fine after Clucky's visit."

"Clucky couldn't know."

"What? What more is there to know, Abbie? Tell

me. These bits and pieces of revelation are driving me crazy.''

She looked down at the baby sleeping peacefully in his car seat. For a moment Ben thought he saw tears gather in her eyes. But when she finally raised her head to look at him, her eyes were clear, her demeanor controlled.

''I've been counseled not to have children,'' she replied, her voice barely above a whisper. ''The hormonal rush could retrigger my cancer.''

''Abbie!'' His stomach lurched, his equilibrium shattered. Her presence was little less than a minefield.

''Our—'' He caught himself. ''Your plans always included children. You'd make a terrific mother.'' Seeing the unguarded expression on her face, he shut up before he made matters worse.

The fact that she could find the courage to speak of childlessness overwhelmed him. Like an ice floe separating from a glacier, a tiny fragment of bitter reserve broke away from his heart. Instinctively, he moved to put his arms around her.

Her green eyes grew cool as she stiffened and stepped away. ''I'm okay with it.''

''How can you be?''

''It's part of who I am now. It's life.'' She held her chin high.

''It's not fair.''

''As an entitlement, fairness has been oversold.''

''Abbie.'' He wanted to hold her. Wanted her to want to be held.

''Is that pity in your eyes, Ben Chase?''

Pity? No, not pity, but shared pain. He couldn't bring himself to admit that, however.

"No," he said simply.

"Because I don't want your pity," she insisted. "I don't want you to see me as lacking or needy." She squared her shoulders. "As I said earlier, I'm fine."

He began to see beyond the rejection to her vulnerability. "There are lots of things I might feel toward you, Abbie Latham, but pity isn't one of them."

"Ben!" Sully Chase, Ben's second-youngest brother, approached with his three young children in tow.

At any time since Abbie's return, Ben had welcomed interruption. He didn't now. He wanted the world to go away. Wanted to get to the bottom of all Abbie had been through.

"Unca Ben!" His four-year-old niece, Felicity, threw herself at his knees. "Have you seen Santa yet?"

With a nonchalance born of being cool kindergartners, the twins, five-year-olds Nina and Noah, hung back in their enthusiasm.

"We want to see the boat," Nina explained.

"It's Will Denny's," Noah added, glancing at Abbie. "He had it made in Nova Scotia. It doesn't look like Uncle Garrett's."

Sully Chase flat-out ignored Abbie. "Will we see you for supper at Garrett's?" he asked, looking pointedly at Ben.

"I'm not off tonight, but I'll stop in around six for a quick bite to eat." He indicated Abbie with a nod. "Sully, you know—"

"Santa!" Felicity insisted, tugging on Ben's pant-leg. "Have you seen him?"

Attempting an uncle's frown, Ben lifted Felicity. "What happens to little girls who interrupt?"

"Not at Christmas." Felicity had a boldness that reminded Ben of Margot.

"Especially at Christmas."

"Sorry." His niece looked sorry for all of two seconds. "But you're the chief. You know everything. You gotta know when Santa's coming."

"Santa's due in fifteen minutes."

"Daddy, let's go!" Felicity wriggled from Ben's grasp, then seized her brother's and her sister's hands. "Let's get a good spot at the head of the cove!"

"Not without me," Sully cautioned. "See you at Garrett's." He waved at Ben and left without acknowledging Abbie.

"I'm sorry," Ben said, feeling a twinge of Chase disloyalty. "I don't know what got into him." Twice before he'd refused to trash Abbie to family members. And now he found himself taking up for Abbie over Sully. What was happening? He was supposed to be pushing her away. "He was rude." He couldn't avoid the facts.

"I understand how I could get on the bad side of the Chase family. *I'm* sorry. I'm trying to make it clear to you, Ben, how sorry I am."

He felt embarrassment at his brother's insensitive behavior. His own anger at Abbie had declared a temporary truce in light of her most recent revelation. Her survival had come with conditions, but she carried on with a reality-laced optimism. How could you not admire her calm in the face of resistance?

He didn't want to admire her. Admiration would leave him open to her considerable charms. Like her soft rosy lips or her creamy smooth skin.

"You scratched yourself," he said, ignoring her apology, indicating a thin red line along her cheek.

"Ah, Murphy." She looked relieved at the conversation's new direction. "Sometimes he doesn't know his own strength."

"Murphy?"

Fingering the tiny gold pin on her lapel, Abbie grinned. "My guardian angel."

Leave it to Abbie to turn a heavy moment into an upbeat one. She could get him into the darnedest discussions.

"For real?"

"Well, I don't know who my real guardian angel is." Sunlight threaded her red hair with gold. Her green eyes sparkled with an inner light. Did she have any idea how pretty she was? "Murphy's just a reminder."

"Didn't you once tell me you had an old dog named Murphy?"

"Oh, yes. When I was five, he died. No one could console me until Mom told me he was running free, playing Frisbee with the angels."

Bemused, Ben shook his head. "You named your guardian angel after a dog."

"Well, he *was* a watchdog."

Her open smile reminded him he'd always felt uplifted in her presence. Uplifted was one thing. Attracted was another. He couldn't afford attraction.

The woman he'd once known as well as he'd known himself had become an enigma. Despite her revelations, he could sense she kept something more from him. She hadn't trusted him with the full truth eight years ago. She still didn't trust him. Lack of trust canceled out attraction any day.

He needed space. "I need to keep moving."

"I understand." The tilt of her head said she understood far more than he wished. Understood right down into the core of him. As she always had.

He walked away, wondering if the remainder of his days in Point Narrows would be dogged by this push-me-pull-me sensation in the pit of his stomach.

"Mother, this child is not endangering my health." Abbie balanced a fussy Baby on her hip and a cell phone with a fading connection between her ear and shoulder as she searched for a clean creeper amid the stack of used clothing Meg's wise women had brought. Baby had spit up most of his supper on the old one.

"Darling—" Celeste Latham sighed, concern suffusing each syllable "—we only agreed you might return to Maine if you absolutely promised to take care of yourself."

"I am taking care of myself. I feel better right now than I've felt in eight years."

"I was once a mother of an infant, in case you'd forgotten." The cell phone reception deteriorated further. "I know how fatiguing the experience can be."

"It's exhilarating, Mother." Having found a creeper, Abbie tried to maneuver in the tight space between her bed and Baby's portable crib. "Besides, it's only temporary until Janis McDougal can find a more permanent home. And Ben's helping—"

"Ben? Ben Chase?"

"Yes. He's now the police chief." Gently Abbie laid Baby in his crib on the changing pad. "He works closely with Social Services."

"Do you think it wise to reopen that particular relationship?" Celeste admonished, her voice fuzzy from fading cell power.

"I don't mean to reopen anything." The statement was a conflicted half-truth.

"You mustn't…get overwrought."

"I don't intend to get overwrought, Mother. I simply intend to participate in life."

"It's…you and…intense…"

"We're breaking up." In all the activity of moving, Abbie hadn't recharged her cell phone. It was as good a way to end a prickly conversation as any. "I'll call you later."

"Dad…love…"

"I love you, too." Signing off, Abbie turned her attention to Baby. "We need regular phone service in here, yes, we do. But until then, let's see why you're so fussy." She glanced at her watch. Five fifty-five. "Too early to be hungry again."

Unsnapping the creeper, she inhaled sharply at the sight of the bright red rash covering the little one's torso. "Oh, what have we done?"

Taking off the entire garment revealed the rash extended to his arms and legs, which he now waved in an infantile rage. His cries made it fairly impossible to think.

Oh, Baby.

She needed help, and quickly.

Meg Nichelini. She could call Meg. But the cell phone was dead, and she had no regular service.

She spotted a baby care book amid the supplies Meg's crew had brought and lunged for it. Rashes. Redness. She scanned the index, then the chapters, appalled at what she found. Chicken pox. Measles. Scarlet fever. Dear Lord, was it possible? She needed a doctor. The nearest hospital was fifteen miles away.

Baby wailed his discomfort.

Ben! Ben had helped raise four children. He'd know what to do, and if he didn't, he'd make a sure-fire escort to the hospital.

In desperation, she tried her cell phone one more time. Dead. Exasperated, she chucked the thing into the diaper pail.

She'd have to drive to the police station.

Baby's rash looked painful, but she couldn't take him out without covering him. She hadn't lost her mind completely. Her pulse racing, she bundled him loosely in a receiving blanket, then hurried downstairs to find his snowsuit.

"Baby, Baby," she whispered. "Did Janis make a terrible mistake leaving you with me?"

She bit her tongue. She would not entertain negative thoughts.

As she tried to fit the squirming infant into his snowsuit and he fought her at every move, she suddenly remembered Ben saying he'd stop by Garrett's around six for a bite of supper. The Chase family's traditional Saturday night get-together. Garrett lived just down the street from her.

Oh, my. That would be so much closer than either the police station or the hospital.

"Come on, Baby." Having dressed him as best she could, she hastened to her car, without pausing for her own coat. "When I get you to the Chases', everything's going to be all right."

Chapter Seven

The difference between last Saturday and this Saturday was as monumental as the Great Divide. Last Saturday Ben had joined his family for their weekly get-together with a welcome sense of escaping the rough edges of daily life and job. This Saturday, instead of providing a refuge, the Chases surely would exacerbate his troubles, their interest in and opinions on Abbie's return spurring a caustic situation.

Garrett met him at the door. "Glad you could make it."

"Was there any doubt?"

"Margot and Sully said your time's been pretty well taken up with Abbie."

"With the baby, Garrett. With the baby." Ben stepped from the front porch directly into the small living room filled with the noise of Chases in family banter, filled with the scent of evergreen from the fat Christmas tree in the corner.

"Ben!" came the chorused greeting as he hung his jacket on a peg by the door.

"I thought we agreed Abbie Latham was trouble," Garrett muttered under his breath, unwilling to give the subject a rest.

Although used to an acerbic give-and-take with his brothers, Ben reined in a hasty reply. Garrett had just gone through a messy divorce and a successful but ugly custody battle for his six-year-old daughter, Mariah. Ben understood Garrett was presently in a bad place where grown women were concerned.

Instead of rising to his brother's bait, Ben asked, "How's Pop?"

Scowling, Garrett nonetheless let the subject of Abbie drop. "Okay. He's in the kitchen. Only a few beers so far. But the night's early. Go talk to him. Keep him *and you* out of trouble."

Hell, where Abbie was concerned, Ben had found himself mired in trouble long before he'd realized he was sinking. His family needn't know that.

He made his way through the press of Chase adults and children. Around the coffee table, Margot, their eighteen-year-old brother, Jonas, Sully and his wife, Candace, played a heated game of cribbage while Ben's young nieces and nephew Mariah, Felicity, Nina and Noah watched an animated Christmas video. When the adults motioned him to join them, he waved them off with, "Gotta talk to Pop."

Garrett tailed Ben as if he weren't old enough to make it through to the kitchen without getting in a jam, as if he hadn't bailed the lot of them out of more than one sticky situation. They hadn't questioned his common sense or his maturity then. He didn't like the feeling that they were trying to take care of him now.

The oldest of the five siblings, Ben had helped Pop hold the family together through the early years, then helped the other kids keep Pop off the bottle later. Pop did okay most of the time.

Garrett had said their father had consumed only a few beers. Maybe he wouldn't get to the hard stuff tonight. Maybe. The news of Abbie's return, however, might trigger painful memories. Might remind Tobias of Sandra's leaving. Tobias had been the most vocal in his anger when Abbie had left his son eight years ago. He'd taken the rejection personally. It had been an old hurt reactivated. While Ben had seen through the anger to the sorrow, Tobias Chase was not an easy man to comfort.

He'd grown more laconic and distant with each passing day. A master carpenter, he abstained from drink on the job. Abstained from friendships too. His only solace, if you could call it that, came from family. And even family he didn't let close enough emotionally to effect any real healing. The past hovered about Tobias like a bad winter cold, invisible except for the unhealthy effects.

Perhaps it could be said three of the Chase men were not in a good place where grown women were concerned.

At the kitchen table Ben slid into a seat opposite his father while Garrett checked the pots on the stove. The comforting aroma of chowder and skillet corn bread spread through the room as he lifted lids.

"Pop." Ben nodded to his father and waited for the diatribe against Abbie.

"Ben." Tobias took a swig from his beer bottle, holding firm with his usual disinclination to talk.

Ben took advantage of his father's silence to direct the conversation. "How's the Pennyman place coming?" Tobias and crew were building a luxury home on the Pier Road for summer residents.

"It's work. A little rich for my tastes, though."

Garrett turned from his culinary ministrations. "Pop, you know Abbie Latham's back in town."

"Ayuh." Tobias took another swig of beer as Ben sent Garrett an evil glare. "It's none of my business."

The brothers gaped at each other in openmouthed shock.

"Nor none of yours, either." Tobias stared pointedly at Garrett.

Ben could have hugged his father, but that would risk expulsion from the Chase fraternity of undemonstrative males. Once upon a time, Abbie, with her candor and her constant reaching out, had helped to soften what she called his strong, silent New England posture. When she left, she took with her the tools necessary to crack through that veneer.

In lieu of a hug, he stared at his father.

Pop was full of surprises tonight. Ten minutes ago Ben could have bet the boatyard Tobias would come down hard on Abbie. But here he sat, refusing to get involved and insisting Garrett butt out, as well. The cop in Ben grew suspicious.

But he grinned at Garrett all the same. "I'll have that soft drink you were about to offer me." At this point he welcomed an upper hand, no matter the source.

"You can run, but you can't hide," Garrett growled, pulling a can from the fridge.

The doorbell rang.

"I'll get it." Ben rose, glad to stretch, glad to step out of the kitchen away from the emotional jabs precipitated by his father's unexpected behavior. As much as Garrett gnawed on the subject of Abbie like an old dog with a worn-out bone, he was transparent in his obsession. Ben could appreciate his brother for his predictability. What a sad state of affairs.

Before he made his way through the living room, Margot opened the door. Silence fell on the room as every Chase stared at the newcomer.

Coatless, Abbie stood in the doorway, the heavily bundled baby in her arms, a stricken look on her face.

After one long moment of stunned silence, the air filled with Baby's complaints.

"What's wrong?" Ben physically moved Margot aside to make room for Abbie to enter the warmth of Garrett's house. What had possessed her to leave her own house without a coat?

"I don't know what's wrong," she replied. "Baby has a terrible rash all over his body."

"Oh, my goodness! The children!" Sully's wife moved toward the four kids as if by that effort alone she could prevent contagion.

"Relax, everyone." Ben took the infant from Abbie's arms. "Babies get rashes." He didn't bring up the fact that they had no medical records for this foundling, no proof that he was indeed healthy. No use fueling panic. "Let's take a look at you, big guy.'' He touched Baby's forehead with the back of his hand. ''No fever.''

Worry written all over her face, Abbie hastily undid the child's snowsuit as Ben held him and the Chases looked on in judgmental silence.

When Abbie pushed aside the underlying cotton blanket, Ben immediately noted the rash confined to the baby's torso, arms and legs. ''It could be prickly heat,'' he said. ''How heavily have you kept him clothed?''

''Except when I took him outdoors, I've kept him in lightweight creepers.'' She gently brushed her hand over the fussy child's downy head. ''I wrapped him in the blanket to bring him here because even the creeper seemed to bother him.''

''Was it one of the creepers that came with him?''

''No.'' Abbie huddled so close to him and the baby Ben could smell alarm mixed with the woodsy scent of shampoo in her hair. ''It was one of those Meg brought. From the church thrift shop.''

''Did you wash them before you used them?'' Ben asked.

''No. Meg said they were used but clean.''

Rolling her eyes dramatically, Margot snorted.

Abbie blanched. ''Did I do something wrong?''

''We can rectify it,'' Ben assured her. ''He may have had an allergic reaction to the detergent the original owner of the creeper used. Babies often don't react well to changes.''

''What do we do?''

Margot's eyes flashed at Abbie's use of the word *we*. ''*You* can give the clothing the rinsing you should have given them in the first place—''

"I'll help you." With a quick, hard glance at his sister, Ben took a stand. "Does the house have a washer and dryer?"

"Yes."

"Come on. We'll take care of this guy's wardrobe, then we'll give him a baking soda bath to soothe the rash. But first we need to take care of you."

"Me?" Without consideration for herself, she stood there, coatless. That she'd thought first of this helpless infant made an old admiration sneak back into his opinion of her. She'd always exhibited an incredible empathy for others.

"Here, sis." He placed the squirming infant in Margot's arms. "Make yourself useful."

Margot's mouth curved gently and her eyes took on an unaccustomed softness as she held the little boy. A prickly individual herself, she appeared undeterred by the fuss he put up.

Ben reached for his officer's jacket on the peg near the door. "Parents need to take care of themselves so they can take care of the children," he said gruffly, slipping the jacket around Abbie's shoulders, trying not to let her present fragility rattle him.

"Foster parent," she amended.

"No difference." He turned to his family. Their eyes told him Abbie could and should handle the situation on her own now that she knew what to do. They warned her off and warned him to remain where he belonged. "Garrett," he said, knowing full well they'd see his decision as defiance, "I'm borrowing your mackinaw."

Garrett stood in the kitchen doorway, hands on hips, and said nothing. Pop shot Ben an inscrutable look from the kitchen table. Candace hovered over the children like a ruffled hen over her endangered brood. Sully looked…sullen. Only Jonas showed no signs of hostility. Worse, he appeared to harbor a decidedly masculine interest in Abbie's presence.

Ben slapped an unbidden surge of possessiveness back into line.

Margot, now cooing, had managed to soothe the baby.

"You're not bad at this, kiddo." Ben scooped the tyke from her arms. "If this gets out, however, your dragon queen image is shot."

His sister stuck her tongue out at him.

"Real mature," he replied, shaking his head and ushering Abbie to the door. "See if we let you baby-sit."

No sooner had he closed the door on the Chases than he realized what he'd done.

He'd crossed the line.

He'd allied himself with Abbie over the obvious displeasure of his family.

He'd done it for all the right reasons. Because he genuinely cared about Baby's welfare. To prevent Abbie from bothering an overworked Janis McDougal. So that Abbie, benefiting from his experience tonight, wouldn't need so much supervision in the future.

He didn't need her misinterpreting his actions. As she might have with the kiss.

"I'm doing this for the baby," he said, his words gruff when he'd intended them to be professional.

"I know," she replied softly.

He felt instant remorse that he might have hurt her

feelings, then irritation at himself because, against his better judgment, he cared how she felt.

In the short walk to her car, Abbie welcomed the comfort and warmth of Ben's jacket. It protected her not so much from the weather as from his change in mood. A cold front had suddenly passed over his former warm regard, creating a decidedly unsettled atmosphere in its wake.

"I feel like a fool," she admitted. "Surely I could have found prickly heat or allergic reaction in that baby book. But I panicked."

"You did the right thing." His features unreadable, he opened her car door, then snapped Baby into the car seat. "The Chases have raised enough kids and grandkids to provide some answers."

"I was looking for you. Specifically."

He straightened and stared at her for so long she felt she could count each and every one of his thick, dark eyelashes in the street-lamp light.

"Well, you found me," he said at last, his expression losing some of its wintry detachment. Rounding the car, he held the passenger door open for her. "I'll drive. You look like you could use a break."

His face showed little emotion, but the simple gesture of driving her, on top of the loan of his jacket, brought a lump to her throat.

He used to say he'd always take care of her.

But she hadn't returned to Point Narrows to be taken care of.

Having been a patient for eight years, having people minister to her body in ways that left no privacy and very little dignity, she'd thought what she wanted most was space and a chance at independence. Had schooled herself to think as much. But Ben's small protective acts made her reconsider.

They drove to her cottage without speaking. Baby complained in fits and starts from the back seat. Despite Baby's fussing and Ben's silence, Abbie felt more at peace than she had in years. She felt as if she was again truly part of the hurly-burly of life, felt as if she could make a difference this time around. Helping Baby and bringing Ben around to friendship was a start.

Once inside the cottage, Ben took over with amazing efficiency. He gathered up the donated baby clothing and threw a load in the washer. Lacking an infant's bathinette, he showed Abbie how to create a safe bath by lining the bottom of Lily Arrondise's old claw-footed tub with a folded towel and then adding only a couple inches of tepid water in which he'd mixed baking soda to soothe Baby's rash. He even laid a towel over the enormous cast-iron radiator, to warm for use after the bath. Attentive, he now knelt beside Abbie as she lowered Baby into the tub.

"Keep your hand under his head," he cautioned, "and the washcloth over his lower body."

"Why—"

No sooner had Baby's back touched the water than he treated them to a salute that would have made the harbormaster's fireboat proud.

"Too late." Ben chuckled. "A healthy male baby reaction to a change in temperature or texture. We used to say Jonas could extinguish the moon."

Trying to concentrate on a very slippery Baby, Abbie nonetheless caught the affection in Ben's voice.

What a terrific father he'd make. The thought pulled at her ever-childless heartstrings.

"Because he has a rash, don't wash with the cloth." He handed her a plastic cup. "Pour the water gently over his body."

When Abbie did as Ben instructed, Baby cooed and flailed his arms and legs in obvious delight.

"He's a sensuous little guy," she noted.

"Most babies are."

Ben's voice close to Abbie's shoulder reminded her of a much bigger guy whose sensuality had carried her away so many years ago.

"Don't prolong the bath," he advised, unaware of her wandering thoughts. "You don't want him to get chilled." He pulled the towel off the radiator. "I'll dry him while you get his bottle ready."

Abbie lifted Baby out of the bath and placed him in Ben's towel-draped arms. She pushed back a sudden and unexpected wave of yearning as she watched Ben's large, powerful hands cradle the tiny boy. She was shocked to see longing in Ben's eyes as he hummed a ragged lullaby while gently pressing the toweling to Baby's body. Baby hung on every off-key note.

She felt like an outsider, like a child with no coins, standing with her nose pressed to the candy-store window.

"I'll get his bottle," she said, fighting off a self-pity that would do no one any good.

Mentally lecturing herself all the way, she descended to the kitchen. Meg had warned her not to get too attached to Baby, because his presence in her life would prove fleeting. She should have also warned against a reattachment to Ben. His presence was predicated on Baby's and was no less temporary. She reminded herself that the look of longing in his eyes just now had been for Baby, not for Abbie.

He'd been good with his siblings when they were children. He'd be good with his own children. She, on the other hand, would not have children. It was a choice born of research and consultation. Anyone with an ounce of common sense could figure out how unfair it would be to Ben if she should act upon her reawakened attraction to him.

Downstairs, she threw the rinsed load of baby clothes into the dryer and wished she could as easily launder her troubling thoughts.

"Murphy, Murphy." She sighed, warming a bottle of formula in a pan of water on the stove. "What happened to my quest for balance?"

"What did happen to it?"

Abbie whirled to see Ben standing in the kitchen doorway, holding Baby wrapped in a cotton receiving blanket. His eyes told her his question wasn't rhetorical.

So as not to look at him, she shook the bottle of formula, then tested it on her wrist.

"Is Baby too much for you?" he asked, taking a seat in the rocker by the stove.

"No!"

"Then what?"

She handed him the bottle. "How can I explain this?" She paused. "For years I've practiced a calm acceptance of life. But now I realize how much of that self-possession came as the result of my parents and my doctors sheltering me."

Ben offered the bottle to Baby, who suckled greedily. "You're saying you've returned to the real world and it's knocked you off balance?"

"Yes."

"Because of Baby?"

She took a deep breath and remembered her pledge to speak the truth. "Because of you."

He looked directly at her, but said nothing. Because of his silence, she knew he understood her perfectly. She almost wished he'd question her.

But he understood without another word spoken.

They'd connected. Again.

The flicker in the depths of his eyes told her he might feel a fraction of the imbalance she felt.

He adjusted the bottle for Baby. "How long ago did you feel you'd beaten cancer?"

His question threw her off guard. "Why...seven years ago I received my first cancer-free report."

"Did you think to contact me then?"

"I did," she admitted. "But I couldn't."

Hurt crinkled the fan of lines at the outer edges of his eyes. "Why not?"

"I've spent seven years holding my breath. Praying the cancer wouldn't return." She leaned back against the secure edge of the counter. "I couldn't ask you to do the same."

A muscle twitched along his jaw. "Why not?"

"Ben, you don't seem to understand that I live one day at a time."

He held her with his unwavering blue-gray gaze. "Don't we all?"

"It's not the same."

"No, it isn't." He gently rocked Baby in the old

chair, but his eyes were not gentle. They were flinty
and determined, as if he meant to communicate some
hard fact. "I go to work every morning and try not
to think this might be the day I get caught in the cross
fire of a domestic dispute. Garrett tries not to think
he and his boat could be in deep trouble with a change
in the weather. Sully's a lineman. I don't need to tell
you about those storm-downed wires. Pop drinks too
much. We all try not to worry about his heart—"

"I get your point, but—"

"No *buts*. All of us court some danger in life. None
of us can predict the future. We take a deep breath
and get through the day."

That he was right made her cheeks sting, made a
prickly heat run through her hairline. Illness hadn't
bestowed upon her alone the imperative to live in the
present.

The bottle empty, Ben lifted Baby to his shoulder,
where Baby emitted a tremendous belch.

"Goodness!" Abbie exclaimed in surprise. "He
seems proud of himself!"

"Of course. He's a self-satisfied male." Ben nearly
smiled, but caught himself. His expression quickly returned to sober. "There's no future more precarious
than Baby's. You don't see him holding back."

"He's just a baby."

Ben stood. "The lesson's still the same." He
handed a well-fed Baby to Abbie.

"I'm sorry," she said, clutching the tiny bundle of
warmth and utter trust. She looked Ben squarely in
the eyes. "I underestimated you eight years ago."

They stood almost toe-to-toe, the baby between
them. The look of longing returned to Ben's eyes. He

leaned closer, and Abbie could almost taste his lips upon hers. Against all good sense, she would welcome his kiss.

But his kiss was not for her.

Ben lowered his head and brushed his lips across one of Baby's hands. "Sleep tight, big guy, and don't let those bedbugs bite."

Holding firmly to Baby, Abbie ran the tips of her free hand along Ben's temple. "What does it mean to you to hear I'm truly sorry?" she whispered.

He started, then straightened and backed away. "What does it mean to me?" His expression turned stony. "Nothing. I don't deal in *what ifs*." He made for the door. "I have to make rounds."

Abbie watched him leave. He seemed further from her now than at any time since her return. But she understood his denial and his pain. Having walked a similar route, she had a big decision to make. If she were to help Ben let go of his unresolved anger, she might seriously jeopardize her own hard-won emotional balance.

She glanced at Baby, who now dozed contentedly after having put two adults through their paces. He certainly knew how to get what he wanted, what he needed, and still find peace in the end. As she rocked him, her heart swelled with affection.

Suddenly she remembered something her grandmother used to say. She'd tell Abbie the sweetest fruit hangs on the farthest reaches of the tree. To grasp the fruit, you must be willing to go out on a limb.

She'd gone out on a limb for Baby. If she were honest with herself, she'd admit she'd do the same for Ben. In a heartbeat.

Chapter Eight

"You just missed Abbie." Tabitha, the grocery cashier, grinned up at Ben. "She was in a minute ago, buying throat lozenges. You suppose she's okay?"

Scowling, he handed over the correct change for his doughnuts and coffee, a midmorning snack he wasn't sure his agitated stomach would welcome.

"I don't know a thing about Ms. Latham's health." And he didn't know why he was supposed to care. But ever since Abbie had returned to town, every Point Narrows resident inquired after her as if he had intimate knowledge of her every move.

The probings were beginning to have a direct effect on his stomach acids.

"Ms. Latham, is it?" Tabitha feigned surprise. She'd gone to high school with both Ben and Abbie. "My, how times have changed."

"Hey, leave Ben alone." The welcome voice of his best friend, Dante Nichelini, boomed over Ben's left shoulder. "He's had a hard night chasing rats at the dump."

"Rats at the dump?" Slitting his eyes, Ben turned to Dante. "When I get no respect, I start looking through the Boston papers for police department openings."

"Oh, don't do that!" Tabitha exclaimed. "We haven't even seen how your reunion with Abbie's going to play out."

"It's played out." Ben scooped his purchases off the counter. "And it's times like these I wish we·had a law on the books—a real stiff law—against nosiness."

"But we don't." Tabitha clearly saw the reprimand as banter. "So live with it, Chief."

Shaking his head, Ben headed for the exit. So much for thinking he could run an easy errand just because Margot wasn't on duty.

"Hold up." Dante handed Tabitha a bill. "I'm eating on the run, too. Might as well sit in the parking lot together. Your cruiser or my Jeep?"

"Your Jeep smells like bait."

"Specimens, Ben. Specimens." Dante was a marine biologist. "So we'll sit in your cruiser."

"Seems as if two good-looking guys like you would have better things to do than keep each other company over doughnuts and coffee in a grocery-store parking lot." Tabitha's best customer-service feature was her ability to needle with a New England tenacity.

"I have better things to do. Ben doesn't," Dante replied with a grin. "So I have to counsel the guy."

Despite the razzing, Ben was glad to see Dante. Older by seven years, this particular friend had experienced his own ups and downs with women. Well, *woman*. There had only ever been one woman for Dante, and she was Meg, his wife. But the difficulties they'd experienced in attaining happily-ever-after made Dante as good a candidate as any for a sounding board.

Not that Ben considered pursuing happily-ever-after with Abbie.

Not at all.

He simply needed to sort out the conflicting feelings that had shaken him since he'd seen her in front of Lily Arrondise's cottage Friday morning.

The two men slid into the cruiser at the same time. Although Ben had a dozen different issues rattling around in his brain, needing to find a vent, Dante spoke first.

"You seemed to let Tabitha's teasing get to you just now. Want to talk about it?"

"We're short staffed, and I'm trying to find a baby's missing mother."

"You've handled more than that."

"Yeah. Well, there's Abbie, too."

"Abbie Latham." Dante took a bite out of his doughnut. After chewing thoughtfully, he delivered the zinger. "I don't know the woman, but I know you. And you have the look of a man who maybe cares for her."

"It's not as easy as that." Ben peered into his

doughnut bag. Despite an active morning, he found his hunger had dissipated.

"Why not?"

"You wouldn't know the history. You didn't go to Point Narrows High."

"I've heard rumors, all the same."

Ben looked at Dante in surprise. "You never said anything."

"Figured it wasn't any of my business."

"I wish the rest of the town—my family included—felt the same."

"Now that I see how it's got you balled up inside, maybe I should make it my business."

"It's a long story."

"I have time." Dante grinned. "Meg's Christmas shopping in Portland. Seth's baby-sitting Ariana."

Ben felt a quick stab of envy. Dante had Meg and Seth and Ariana. Ben, on the other hand, had a contrary family, a nosy community and a sporadic love life. He'd never committed to one special woman after Abbie. The fact gnawed at him, emphasizing his solitary emotional existence.

He wanted what Dante had.

"So how did Abbie get under your skin?" Dante's prod brought Ben's thoughts back in line.

"I met her in high school. Junior year. There were never two people more different. I was into sports. Big time. She was into anything academic. The debate team. The literary club. Student government. She was class valedictorian. Brains and Brawn they used to call us. Or Beauty and the Beast, depending who you talked to." One corner of his mouth twitched upward. "The first day I saw her in chemistry class, I fell.

Hard. My knees felt as if they were going to buckle right out from under me.''

''How long did you date her?''

''For the rest of high school, we were inseparable.''

''College split you up, then?''

''Not at all. We both went to the University of Southern Maine. Those four years only brought us closer.'' He winced. ''Or so I thought.''

''What happened?''

''Just before graduation—I'd been accepted as a trainee in the police department here while Abbie had signed a contract as assistant librarian in the elementary school—Abbie disappeared. With her parents.''

''Her parents, too?''

''They put their house on the market and left no forwarding address.''

''Did you ever find out why?''

''This weekend I did.'' Ben caught himself. He didn't feel comfortable airing Abbie's situation, didn't know how much she wanted kept private. But the whole weekend had caught up to him, and he might explode if he didn't unload on some unbiased soul. Dante wouldn't spread tales and he wouldn't judge. ''She had cancer. Thought she might die.''

Dante whistled low, under his breath. ''And she wanted to spare you.''

Ben felt shock that Dante saw immediately what Abbie had tried to make him see. ''That's what she says.''

''But you're not buying.''

''She shut me out. It hurts.''

''Sins of omission.'' Frowning, Dante looked away. ''I've been guilty there.'' He looked back at

Ben. "Don't be too hard on her. She's back. Maybe she's trying to put things right. Give her time and space."

"I'd like to give her space, but this baby left on the library doorstep has us thrown together."

"That should get you talking. Who knows what you might reopen."

"That's just it." Ben glared through the windshield at the snow starting to fall in heavy, wet flakes. "I'm not so sure I want to reopen anything. In fact, I don't want to spend a minute more than necessary with the woman."

"Why not?"

"I'm only going to say this once, and then you're going to forget it." He didn't want to say it even once, but if he didn't get it off his chest, it might crush him. "When I'm with her, it's as if the past eight years didn't exist."

"You want her that bad?"

"Worse."

"What keeps you from going after her?"

Pride.

"I haven't a clue as to how she feels about me." That was only half-true. He knew how she'd felt in his arms when he'd kissed her. She'd kissed him back. With passion. And the reciprocating passion he'd felt clear down to his toes rocked his belief that he wanted nothing more to do with her romantically.

"One minute she seems…interested," he continued. "The next she retreats. Seems as if she needs nothing and nobody. There's something untouchable about her. She opened up enough to tell me she had cancer, but I get the feeling she's leaving something unsaid.''

"Sounds as if she might be as balled up as you," Dante offered. "Talk to her. More important, listen to her."

"I gotta make rounds," Ben snapped. "There's a nor'easter headed this way. Loaded with snow. You got your boat pulled up?"

"Yeah. I took care of it this morning." Dante eyed him cautiously. "You've got some conversation-stopping technique. You use that on Abbie?"

Ben thought of how he'd shut her down last night when she'd asked what it meant to have her say she was sorry. It wasn't his finest moment. "Too often," he muttered.

"You're going to give yourself an ulcer if you don't clear the air with her. Be honest with her. Be honest with yourself."

Ben winced. How could he be honest with Abbie? He hadn't been honest with himself.

Dante opened the cruiser door. "Stop by for dinner one of these nights. Meg and the kids would love to see you."

"Thanks. Maybe I will."

"Bring Abbie and the baby."

"You're pushing it, Nichelini."

Outside the car, the door still open, Dante bent to glance inside. "Take it from a guy who's learned from experience. As painful as this unsaid thing is between you and Abbie, it's not going to go away until you get it out in the open."

Ben grunted a nonresponse, then turned the key in

the ignition, hoping Dante would get the hint. He'd officially closed the subject of Abbie Latham.

Dante took the hint and shut the door.

"If the subject is closed, why am I still thinking about her?" Ben muttered to himself as he pulled the cruiser out of the grocery-store parking lot.

Baby, alert in his car seat on the charge desk, kept Abbie company as she puttered in the library. This quiet Sunday morning seemed a perfect time to get a feel for the collection before she began her transitional internship with Pat Spenser tomorrow. While the library was closed, Abbie wanted to revel in the prospect of her new job, wanted to savor the reason she'd returned to Point Narrows.

If the truth be told, she wanted a bit of a retreat from Lily Arrondise's cottage, a place that had meant so much to two dreamy kids, a place that was beginning to forge memories for two conflicted adults.

If only Ben hadn't kissed her in the cottage.

If only he hadn't so tenderly helped her care for Baby there.

If only he hadn't left his scarf behind in his haste to avoid her question last night. It was a standard issue police scarf, but it was redolent of Ben. Foolishly, she'd slept with it underneath her pillow.

Yes, she needed to take a break from fantasy and concentrate on books and Internet connections and charge systems. Once her mind broke clear of unrealistic romantic cobwebs, she could begin to form a plan to help Ben get beyond the buried anger she knew he still harbored deep within. Issues of abandonment. He needed to learn to let go, and she was a veteran of letting go.

She'd help him because he was another human being in pain, not because she could fall in love with him all over again. Falling in love did not show up on her itinerary to a balanced life.

Sorting through the children's collection, pulling holiday books for display, Abbie came across an old childhood favorite. "Oh, Baby!" she exclaimed. *"Runaway Bunny!"* A warmth of remembrance washing over her, she settled on the edge of the checkout desk and showed Baby the colorful cover. "You're never too young to hear this story."

Eyes wide, Baby cooed his pleasure.

"Ben's not watching. You can cut the act."

Startled, Abbie looked up to see Margot Chase standing in the doorway.

"I beg your pardon?"

Margot stood with arms crossed, her expression as confrontational as her words. "Everyone knows the only reason you agreed to care for this baby is so you can lure Ben into your trap."

Abbie took a deep breath to prevent a caustic rejoinder. Now was as good a time as any to practice neutralizing that Chase negativity. Here stood a woman who, from puberty, hadn't received the benefit of a mother's guidance, a woman who'd grown up in the company of rough-and-tumble males. Now Abbie was going to give Margot the benefit of the doubt that she didn't understand the more sensitive exchanges between women.

Remembering how Margot had softened considerably last night when she'd held Baby, Abbie picked him out of his car seat, then walked over to stand before her.

"You held him," she said, offering him again. "Can you say I'm guilty of anything more than falling under the spell of baby magic?"

Margot kept her arms crossed. "You know how Ben feels about kids."

"That's why Janis McDougal asked him to supervise me. And then Meg Nichelini brought over a crew to help. It's really a community effort. You could be part of it, too, if you wanted."

The look in Margot's eyes said the offer tempted her, but the temptation was not as strong as her bitter grudge. "What I want is for you to butt out of Ben's life."

"Because of Baby, I can't at the moment."

"But you can when the baby's gone to a more permanent foster home."

"That's for Ben to decide, Margot." Abbie strove to keep her voice calm.

She didn't want to back down in front of Margot, but she didn't want to antagonize her. She definitely wanted to keep the lines of communication open. Smiling at Baby, who attempted to smash his thumb in his mouth, Abbie let the residual from that smile rest on Margot. "I didn't come back to hurt him again."

"Why did you come back?"

"Because Point Narrows never stopped being home."

"Then why did you leave?"

Abbie didn't feel comfortable opening up to a hostile Margot. Maybe sometime in the future Ben's sister would open herself up to another's pain, but not today.

"For the moment," Abbie said, "let's just say I had some very important private issues to deal with."

"Oh, my." Margot stuck her nose in the air. "Lathams always were so rich and important we common folk couldn't possibly understand their private issues."

"I'm really sorry you don't like me. There was a time I thought we could be close. Neither of us had a sister—"

"Don't give me family dynamics," Margot snapped, so quickly Abbie realized she'd hit a sore spot. "I never needed a sister. I never needed a—" She stopped, her eyes flashing. "I never needed a Latham feeling sorry for me."

Abbie could have sworn Margot had almost slipped and said she didn't need a mother. In an instant, Abbie began to see how Baby's abandonment might upset Margot as much as Abbie's return. Compassion on Abbie's part made patience easier.

"I don't feel sorry for you." She shifted Baby on her shoulder, gaining confidence from his warmth and her new insight. "In fact, I always admired you."

Margot rolled her eyes.

"I admired your fight. You see, I've only just learned to fight."

"Is that a threat?" Margot bristled. "Because if you're threatening me, I'll—"

"You'll do what, Margot Elizabeth?" Ben's deep voice startled both women, neither of whom had noticed his entrance. He strode across the small library and, in a proprietary gesture, scooped Baby out of Abbie's arms. "Hey, big guy."

With Baby settled in the crook of his elbow, Ben leveled a stare at Margot. "What were you about to do? I'm interested."

"Butt out," Margot sputtered.

Ben cocked one eyebrow in warning.

"I have to agree with your sister," Abbie cut in. "Although I wouldn't have put it quite so... succinctly. Margot and I were ironing out some differences. No referee needed."

Although she secretly relished Ben's renewed presence in her life, Abbie had learned to fight her own battles, to strike her own bargains. Because Ben was a strong individual with a compelling personality, there was inherent danger in letting him come to her rescue. A woman could let a man like him slip into her life on a resurrected wave of attraction and then find she was in over her head. Way over her head. Pulled out to sea on a riptide.

Wary, Ben looked from Abbie to Margot.

Margot seemed in no hurry to reveal the gist of their discussion. Moreover, she eyed Abbie with a glimmer of respect. Abbie had a suspicion Margot Chase wouldn't countenance tattlers.

"We're cool," Margot said with a toss of her head. "For now."

"For sure?" Ben eyed her with a big brother's authority.

"Don't let that badge go to your head." Turning on her heel, Margot aimed the parting salvo over her shoulder.

As soon as the library door closed behind his sister,

Ben turned to Abbie. "Are you okay?" Concern softened his handsome features.

"Why wouldn't I be?"

"Margot's got a wicked tongue."

"As she said, we're cool." Abbie flashed him a grin. "Sticks and stones, and all that."

"I feel as if I should apologize for my whole family. Last night they weren't at their best. Sully was rude in the square—"

"Let it go." She knew how hard it was for him to step outside family loyalty. "I have."

"So easily?"

"Nothing's easy about letting go. But the rewards are great." She reached out her finger so Baby could grasp it. "Only if you're a baby can you hang on for dear life. Did you stop in to check on this bruiser? He's getting bigger and stronger before our very eyes."

"I saw Margot's car and stopped in to check on you."

"Are you hovering, Ben Chase?"

"No!" His neck grew red. "I just didn't think you should get agitated." He scowled. "In your condition."

His words cut deep. In an instant, her worst fears were realized. He saw her not as an individual, but as a cancer patient.

Her disease, even in remission, posed an obstacle she loathed.

"I won't break," she said simply.

The startled look in his eyes said he'd realized his misstep. "I didn't mean—"

"What did you mean?" She hoped the revelation

of her illness hadn't turned her into some china doll in Ben's eyes.

"You talked about coming home for balance." Ben jiggled Baby gently until he gurgled with pleasure. "There's nothing like Margot for rocking the boat."

"Perhaps my boat needs a little rocking." What would Murphy say? Were seizing and rocking synonymous? "The ups and downs are part of life," she continued thoughtfully. "For so long I've concentrated on staying safely in that boat. I've lived and breathed survival. Perhaps it's time I took a chance and got wet."

"Are we still talking about Margot? I got lost in the metaphor. You were the lit major, remember."

Abbie grinned. "Margot and I need to work out a few things, yes. But we can do it on our own. A little disagreement won't hurt me."

"She always had an independent streak, that Abbie Latham," Ben confided to Baby. "I was going to warm up her car for her when she was ready to leave, but I know now she'd rather do it herself."

He nuzzled Baby's nose. The little boy's eyes crossed.

"Baby would love a warm car, thank you very much." Swiping her keys off the desk, Abbie handed them to Ben. "We're just about finished here. It's Baby's lunchtime. I'd appreciate the help."

The incident with Margot had been a small thing, as was Ben's idea to warm up her car. But Abbie wanted to make it clear to Ben—and to herself—that she was capable of handling life's difficulties on her own, and at the same time she would make decisions when and if to accept help. If Ben and she were not to be lovers, she certainly didn't want him as a patronizing big brother. She wanted a relationship based on a mutual respect. A respect for their individual ability to make choices.

"So you won't accept my help with Margot, but you will let me warm up the car." He wrapped his hand as much around her hand as around the keys she offered. His touch conveyed great strength. If she didn't need to lean on herself, it would be so easy to lean on him. "Go figure."

"You don't have to go figure." She tilted her head saucily and looked him right in the eye. "You only have to ask."

As the warmth from Abbie's hand crept into his, Ben released her. Ask. Easy for her to say. For him, asking and telling were two of the most difficult tasks you could put before him. They were such emotional activities. She wasn't talking police investigation here. That kind of asking was a snap. She was talking personal revelation. He'd given that up eight years ago.

He handed Baby to Abbie, then left the library to start and warm her car. Although the snow still fell in wet, ragged flakes, making it a raw noon, the nor'easter had stalled off the coast, sending threat and bluster instead of consummation.

Ben slid behind the wheel of Abbie's car. Before turning the key in the ignition, he looked through the windshield, through the library's front window rimed with frost to where Abbie stood holding the baby, watching him. With the library lights forming a back-lit glow, the mother-and-child tableau nearly took his breath away.

He fisted his hand against the steering wheel. He could kick himself for bringing up her cancer earlier. He came off sounding as if he thought of her as some kind of invalid. Fragile. Maybe if he were honest with himself, he'd admit it was safer to force her into a stereotype than it was to allow himself the freedom to see her as she really appeared to him. Provocative. Sensuous. And far too desirable.

He reminded himself that, for whatever reasons, she hadn't considered him worthy of partnering her through the darkest moments of her life. Even now, after he'd ticked off his family by supporting her, she didn't want his help.

She'd retreated to untouchable mode.

Dante would tell him to ask her what she did want. To still the nagging ache around his heart, he'd get around to asking, even though he bet he wasn't going to like the answer. Hell, at least he'd get closure.

When he turned the key in the ignition, the car failed to respond. No whining. No grinding. Not a spark of life. As reticent as he felt.

Climbing out of the car, he made a concerted effort not to look at Abbie and the baby. He didn't need fantasy at the moment. He needed cold, hard reality. Grateful for a mundane physical task, he rummaged in the trunk of his cruiser for jumper cables, then carefully made the hookups. Even then, Abbie's car didn't respond. If he had to guess, he'd say a faulty fuel pump was the culprit. Abbie and Baby would need a ride home.

As much as he'd like to have warmed her car and left, a secret, senseless part of him rejoiced in the excuse to prolong the contact.

* * *

She stood on the rise next to the lobster-trap Christmas tree and watched the librarian and the cop get into the patrol car with her baby. Little Justin.

Wasn't that a trip? She'd spent the past three and a half months avoiding cop cars, and here she was grateful for the one swallowing up her son.

Tears stung her eyes. She hadn't wanted to leave him, but the beach house where Tiffany was letting her hide out didn't have heat except for a drafty wood-burning stove. It wasn't any place for a baby.

She coughed a deep, painful, chest-splitting hack. Besides, she'd developed this cold and didn't want to pass it on to Justin.

He was better off with the cop and the librarian. She knew it. But she didn't like it. She missed her son so. He was all she had.

She noticed with satisfaction that the librarian carried him in a car seat, whereas that cheap plastic laundry basket was the best she could manage. She could have gone to Social Services, perhaps. But they'd have asked a lot of questions. As hard up as she was, she didn't need to be answering questions.

Straining to catch a good glimpse of Justin as the cop took him from the librarian then loaded him into the patrol car, she prayed those two strangers were taking good care of her son. Did they know he liked his feet tickled? Did they sing to him as she did? If they did, they probably sang those lame nursery songs she didn't remember the words to. She'd forgotten everything except "Itsy Bitsy Spider," but she knew all the lyrics The Hanky Spanky Crustaceans had ever written. Justin loved her singing.

The patrol car pulled away from the library. She wiped her nose on the sleeve of her jacket. Her head felt as if it were about to explode. The crying didn't help.

Maybe having a baby had been a mistake. No! She pushed the thought from her mind. Justin was her whole life. She was going to get rid of this freakin' cold. She was going to get a job. McDonald's was hiring. She was going to take care of her baby. He was going to grow up to be all she wouldn't be.

"Heather!" Tiffany leaned out of Zeke's car. "You coming, or what?"

"Minute." Heather waved Tiffany off. Maybe after she got better, she'd approach the librarian. The woman seemed kind. She might take her in along with Justin. She seemed cool. Not too old. Maybe she'd understand without too much hassle. And her old man was everything a guy should be, no matter he was a cop. Solid. Protective. Dependable. Not like that jerk Kevin.

It was time to move on. Her toes had grown numb. Besides, musicians and singers were setting up for some kind of concert around the base of this goofy Christmas tree.

Christmas.

Last year at this time her biggest worry had been arguing with her mom for colored lights instead of white, for a vegetarian dinner instead of the usual protein blowout, for the inclusion of 10 Boyz with Chainsaws in the repertoire of holiday CDs on the family stereo. How Mom loved Christmas. Daddy grumbled about the cost, but he wouldn't have it any other way.

The thought of her family grabbed her. Twisted her conscience. She'd let them down. She'd gotten pregnant. She hadn't told them. Before they could kick her out, she'd run.

But, in running, had she let Justin down? It was his first Christmas and he didn't know his grandparents. Her parents—

A tremendous cough racked her body. Sobbing and coughing, she stumbled down the hill toward Zeke's car.

She wanted her baby. She wanted her mother.

Chapter Nine

Later that afternoon, having asked a baby-sitting favor of Meg Nichelini, Abbie strode briskly into the square. She'd try to start her car one more time. If it was indeed dead, she'd call a tow truck and look for a car mechanic in the area yellow pages. No big deal. She knew about real big deals. In comparison, car trouble was just a minor glitch in an otherwise invigorating day. She pulled her hat farther over her ears, then turned her face upward to catch a fat snowflake on her tongue.

As she walked into the square, she couldn't see her car where she'd left it parked in front of the library. Good gracious, had grand auto theft come to sleepy Point Narrows?

Breaking into an anxious jog, she spotted Herbie Thurow pumping gas outside the M & M Hardware.

"Herbie!" she called. "Did you see anyone around my car?"

"Ayuh." Without much wasted effort Herbie turned to replace the gas nozzle on the pump.

"Well, who?" She jogged across the square. "Did you recognize them?"

"Ayuh." Turning to his customer, the pump attendant slowly wiped his hands on his bony rump without offering Abbie any further information.

Her concern rising, she didn't feel up to playing pull-the-gossip-out-of-Herbie. She came to a panting halt before the crusty New Englander. "For pity's sake, Herbie, *who* stole it?"

"Nobody stole it." He bent to the driver's window of the now-gassed-up car. "That'll be eighteen dollars."

"Who took it? Who moved it? Who drove it away?" Two could play this game of semantics. She hopped from foot to foot, now genuinely worried about her car's whereabouts. *"Who?"*

From a greasy roll of bills in his pocket Herbie made change for a twenty. "Chief Chase had it towed away." He gave Abbie a glance that seemed to say, *and that should explain it.* "Thank you kindly," he said to his customer. "Come again."

"Towed away!" Focusing on Herbie, Abbie sidestepped as another car pulled in right after the first, nearly bumping her behind. She was not going to let the laconic pump attendant wait on another customer until she'd found out what he knew about her missing vehicle. To that end she stepped squarely in his path. "Why did Chief Chase tow my car away?"

Forming a gummy grin, Herbie nodded over her shoulder. "Why don't you ask him yourself?"

Abbie whirled around to find herself face-to-face with Ben.

He rested one ungloved hand on a lean hip. "What's the question?"

For a moment, in staring at him, she forgot.

"She wants to know why you towed her car," Herbie chimed in as he moved around the couple to gas up the police cruiser.

"I had it towed to the dealership. For repair first thing tomorrow morning. I thought I'd save you some grief."

"I was going to try to start it again this afternoon."

"That thing was dead."

"So you said earlier." Abbie scowled. "If that was the case, I'd planned to call a tow truck myself. To pick out my own mechanic. Dealerships can be expensive—"

"Mason at the dealership is the best mechanic around," Herbie offered, unasked. "And I think the chief here was just looking out for your best interest."

"I'd have done it for anyone," Ben said, scowling.

"Well, mebbe not," Herbie countered, winking at Abbie. "It helps that the lady's mighty pretty and you two once had that hot thing goin'."

Abbie tried to ignore Herbie's meddling and, instead, looked Ben in the eye. "Thank you for your help. *Again.*" She tried not to sound prim. "But in the future I'd like to have a chance to make my own choices."

"I was just being neighborly." Ben cocked his head as if issuing a challenge. "Perhaps you've been away from small-town life too long to recognize the gesture.''

Still hanging on to the gas nozzle, Herbie craned his neck to catch Ben's attention. "I think, Chief, that Abbie doesn't want to be crowded. You know women these days cherish their independence. Or so I hear on those talk shows.''

"Thank you, Herbie.'' Abbie stuck her hands on her hips. "But I don't need an interpreter.'' She shot Ben her most angelic smile. "Are we clear on this, *Chief?*''

"Let's see.'' Frustration clouded his blue gaze. "You want my advice on the baby. You don't want my advice on my own family. You'll have me warm up your car, but you don't want any emergency road-side assistance.''

"You're making me sound indecisive.'' And prickly, Abbie thought. "I'm not upset when you offer help, as long as you allow me the freedom to accept or decline.''

"Now, Abbie. Try to think with the chief's perspective.'' Herbie screwed the gas cap on the cruiser. "A man's gotta feel useful. Especially around the woman he's sweet o—''

"Herbie!'' Together, Ben and Abbie voiced their exasperation with their conversational shadow.

"Okay!'' Herbie raised his hands in mock surrender. "By thunder, you two are touchy. I'd suggest you lay off the coffee.'' He shook his head, but made no move to leave. "Is this what they call...sexual tension? Heck, this is just like that new cable drama *Twenty*—''

"Put the fill-up on the department's account,'' Ben

muttered, cutting Herbie off. He slid behind the wheel. "And, Abbie, the dealership's in the same place it was when you left town. Same as eight years ago. You should be able to find it. Have them work on your car or not. It's *your choice.*" He shot her a black glower. "I was going to offer you a ride home, but I'm not sure if that's politically correct."

Before Abbie could manage a reply, Ben engaged the ignition, then pulled away from the pumps, leaving her perplexed and openmouthed.

"You hurt his feelings, you know." Herbie sighed.

"Why would his feelings get hurt? Just because I want to make my own choices?"

"Because he was only trying to protect you."

"*Me?* I'm a grown woman. Why would he feel the need to protect me?"

"Because, as I tried to say earlier before you two shushed me, the man's sweet on you." Herbie beamed his pleasure at finally getting that observation out in the open. He then thoughtfully rubbed his stubbly chin with one chapped hand as he watched Abbie and waited for her reaction.

"Herbie, you're a day late and a dollar short. Ben and I are ancient history. We're working together now because Janis McDougal asked us to care for Baby."

"Oh, I didn't say the chief *knows* he's sweet on you again. Realizing he's fallen twice for the same woman in one lifetime would be a hard pill to swallow for any man." The pump attendant scratched his head in deep contemplation. "Course, I don't believe the spark ever went out during those eight years you've been gone. So that would really make it one long fall." He slanted a glance in her direction.

"Considering that, you need to be a little softer with the man."

"I'm already soft. In the head." She tapped her temple. "Listening to your romantic notions."

Perplexed by Ben's behavior and Herbie's intimations, she set off for her cottage. Ben Chase still sweet on her, indeed. The look he'd shot her just now had been sour enough to pickle herring.

But what if there was a grain of truth in Herbie's far-fetched speculation? What if Ben was attracted to her? Even the slightest. Even after he'd learned of her battle with cancer. Even after he'd heard of her choice to remain childless. Wow. Wasn't that the heroic reaction she'd have wished from him? If so, what was to stop them from renewing a romantic attachment now?

She thought of the sensuous physical nature of their former relationship, thought of how freely she'd given of her body, a body then markedly different from her body now. Since Ben and she had last made love, she'd undergone a mastectomy. She'd chosen not to undergo reconstructive surgery. As a single woman, she'd accepted her body. As a prospective lover, well…she felt an intense wariness. It wasn't as if she'd made a conscious commitment to celibacy. It was more that she hadn't courted intimacy.

So, what was to stop her and Ben from reigniting passion?

"You want the truth, Murphy?" In a reflex movement, she ran her fingers over her collar and the angel pin. "I'm not sure I'm sexually attractive, and that scares me where Ben is concerned."

When he'd suggested he'd kissed her to prove their

relationship only ever had been, only ever could be physical, she'd called him on it. They'd always had more. But how much more? She couldn't dismiss the physical attraction as a minor part of their relationship. On the contrary, it had been a major portion of who they were as a young couple.

That they'd experienced deep emotional attachment was her belief. What if he saw only the physical?

Frustration tweaked her. This wasn't one of those issues she could clear up with a straightforward question. Ben and she were still struggling with the process of expressing their everyday wants and needs and hot buttons.

Abbie couldn't see herself standing before Ben in casual conversation, saying, "I had a mastectomy. I chose not to have reconstructive surgery. I have one breast. How does that make you feel?"

Oh, my, it had been difficult enough to bare the truth initially to her support group. But before Ben? He was such a physical man.

"Murph, I'm getting ahead of myself." She laughed aloud. "Do I really want to convince him I can be a sultry temptress? I think I should first convince him I'm not some damsel in distress. Let's see if we can get him to understand I'm capable of handling my own day-to-day affairs. That would be a start in the right direction."

But how to get his attention?

Janis managed with chocolate chip cookies, Margot with hissy fits. Serena had a perfect body…Abbie didn't want to think of Serena's perfect body.

She must concentrate on her gifts, not her deficits. She must be herself. She'd come back to Point Narrows to take control of her life, and here she found herself buffeted by thoughts of two males, Baby and Ben, each of them powerful forces in their own right. The emotional turmoil certainly didn't facilitate her peace of mind. In fact, the boys pulled her in directions she'd chosen not to take. Baby snagged her maternal instincts, while Ben made her blood run hot with yearning. So as not to lose herself on her journey to balanced selfhood, she needed to moderate her reactions to those two.

Perhaps the best reaction was no reaction. No expectations. Danger arose from making mountains out of molehills. Why was she getting agitated? For a fact, she had no clue as to how Ben Chase regarded her.

She exhaled sharply. She needed to let it all go. She'd overreacted.

Ben sweet on her, indeed.

Later that evening, Ben stood on Abbie's doorstep clutching a peace offering, a small, potted fir tree Herbie had guaranteed the freshest on the lot. It was obvious from this afternoon's miscommunication that Abbie and Ben needed to come to an understanding. Herbie's unwanted meddling earlier pointed out that Abbie's and Ben's affairs were increasingly the talk of the town. The gossip had to stop. He would not be the center of idle speculation. But the gossip wouldn't stop if he and Abbie repeated these public discussions. They needed to air their differences and reach middle ground. In private.

And so Ben stood, engulfed in prickly evergreen,

feeling like Father Christmas at a time when he usually felt like Scrooge.

Clutching the heavy pot and hanging on to his pride for dear life, he suppressed an even more bizarre image of himself as an adolescent on a first date. This was *not* a date. And it certainly had nothing to do with hormone-riddled adolescence. He'd dropped in for a meeting between mature adults, to find a consensus for professional communication in the future. The tree was a gesture of goodwill. Nothing more.

Abbie opened the door. The sight of her standing before him, a beatific smile on her face, a crown of tinsel garland in her hair and an antique ornament in her outstretched hand, made all rationalization swirl away with the snowflakes on the next gust of wind.

"Company!" she exclaimed. "Just when I felt in a company frame of mind." Her voice floated on the evening air, light and musical, like holiday bells. "Where did you get that absolutely lovely tree? Baby and I need to get one. We have all Lily Arrondise's ornaments, but no tree."

"This is for you." Self-consciously, Ben muscled the tree through the doorway. "I know how you love Christmas. And I...Herbie thought you might not have a chance, with the baby and all, to get out for a tree."

Abbie's smile widened as she shut the door and shut in the fragrance of fir. "This tree's from Herbie?"

"Well...no." Ben cleared his throat. "Herbie sold it to me."

"For me?"

She knew damn well it was for her. He shifted the

pot in his arms. Although tabletop size, the tree with its balled root proved remarkably heavy. Maybe the gift was a mistake. "I thought you'd like a live tree." He searched for words. "After Christmas you could plant it. Hang food on it for the birds. Watch it grow."

Her eyes glistened as her smile faded from mischievous to pensive. "A gift with a future. How optimistic."

"I only meant—" The full import of her words caught at him. Was he always destined to stray into sensitive territory with this new Abbie? "Maybe you don't—"

"Oh, it's a delightful gift!" She swiped at one eye. "Thank you."

He cleared his throat. "Where do you want it?"

"In the parlor." Her gaze lingered on his face, scrutinizing, before she turned and led the way into Lily Arrondise's company room.

The old-fashioned lamps gave the Victorian velvet furnishings a deep rosy cast, gave the room an almost magical glow. Open boxes of antique ornaments lay everywhere, their contents spilling like jewels over the already cluttered surfaces.

"Isn't this marvelous?" Abbie asked, her face radiant. "The heirs already went through the house and took what had meaning for them. They gave me carte blanche to use the rest. I can't believe no one wanted these ornaments."

Ben felt a tightening in his chest. An unnameable, uncomfortable sensation gripped him.

"There are some very old pieces. It must have taken Miss Lily years to accumulate so many." Her eyes sparkling, Abbie ran her fingers over a delicate blown-glass peacock. "Somehow I don't think she would mind if we celebrated, using her beautiful collection."

The disturbing sensation increased for Ben even as Abbie cleared a space on a sturdy oak table, enabling him to unload the weighty potted fir. "This tree won't hold all those ornaments," he said.

"No way. We'll have to hang the rest around the house."

With her use of *we,* his stomach lurched. He'd intended only the briefest of visits.

Oblivious to his unease, she twirled around in the center of the room, her mounting excitement evident. "We'll make a holiday wonderland with Miss Lily's treasures."

Again, there was that disconcerting *we.*

Suddenly the cause of his misgivings came to him. This room, these ornaments, Abbie's plans for decorating were all so blatantly feminine. In the years after Sandra Chase left, Ben's family had celebrated Christmas, but in a decidedly masculine manner. Lights, practical presents and food. They hadn't gone in for fragile glass ornaments or decorations beyond the tree. Suddenly he felt uneasy, clumsy, a bull in a china shop. Helping Abbie decorate would provide a needed opportunity for them to talk, sure, but at what cost? Remaining in this room made him feel like an outsider, an emotional outsider.

He frowned.

"You will help, won't you?" she asked as if she assumed his answer would be an automatic yes.

"We do need to talk." In fact, he'd come to talk.

Hell, he was man enough to conquer that vulnerable ache. "So…sure." As Abbie blushed, he felt a pull around his heart—this time pleasure mixed with the discomfort. As much as this scene unsettled him, it drew him in.

He shrugged out of his officer's jacket. "Where's Baby?" If they were to talk, he'd welcome all available buffers.

"Asleep. He can't keep his eyes open past seven." She handed him one end of a string of tiny sterling silver bells. "When I put him down for the night, he's good for eight hours. Like clockwork, his internal wake-up comes at three in the morning."

As Ben held one end of the string of bells, Abbie untangled the strand, then looped her end on the little fir's branches. Even in diffused lighting, weariness showed around her eyes.

"You should sleep when Baby does," he offered, concerned she might get overtired, run-down. Sick. He couldn't stand the thought of her sick. "Sully's wife says sleeping when your child does is a luxury first-time mothers have."

Her look grew wistful, but she immediately caught herself. Immediately brightened. "If I were asleep now, I wouldn't be trimming the tree with you."

Although she'd covered nicely, he'd seen the shadow of vulnerability in her eyes when he'd mentioned first-time mothers. She'd said she wouldn't have children. Because of the risks. Because of that damned threat of cancer. Why did he keep sticking his foot in his mouth? She'd gone through so much, he didn't want her to feel uncomfortable around him.

To feel as if each conversation might turn into an emotional minefield. Where was his head?

"I'm sorry I mentioned motherhood. I forgot—" He'd forgotten she wasn't still a twenty-one-year-old woman dreaming dreams of a large family.

"It's okay." Having looped the greater part of the silver string around the tree, she took his end and secured it, as well. The tinkling of the bells underscored the gentle timbre in her voice. "You don't need to tiptoe around me on the topic of children."

He understood she was trying to put him at ease. How Abbie.

A lump rose in his throat as he thought of the joy his nephew and nieces brought to the Chase family. "I don't mean to come off as trying to rub your nose in your situation."

With a sigh she offered him a box from which to choose an ornament. "Baby is enough for now. The children who frequent the library will be enough later." She said it as if she believed it.

Her strength fairly overwhelmed him.

Glad for somewhere to look other than in her accepting eyes, he selected a frosted glass Santa, although he'd rather not decorate a Christmas tree. Abbie's Christmas tree. He'd rather be anywhere else than in this house in which he'd thought he'd spend the rest of his days, with this woman whom he'd wanted—had needed—as his lifelong partner. The direction of their conversation seemed as fragile as these ornaments.

"You can ask me questions, you know," she prompted.

He exhaled sharply with the need to ask her countless questions, with the desire to ask her none. He had to start somewhere, however. They had to work together. For Baby.

Or so he told himself.

"Is it an absolute that you can't have kids?" He couldn't picture sweet, giving Abbie childless.

"No. It's a choice. An educated decision. For me alone. Just like—" She inhaled sharply as if she'd caught herself again. "We always have choices," she continued, her shoulders just a little bit straighter, her chin a little bit higher. "Sometimes we don't like any of the options, but we always have a choice."

"Not always." He scowled. He hadn't had a choice when his mother had walked out. Neither had his father. Or his brothers and sister. That old acid sensation rose in the back of his throat. "Sometimes fate wipes out your options."

"We can always choose our attitude," she replied, touching his forearm in an obvious attempt to draw him toward her way of thinking. "Acceptance is a choice. Happiness is a choice. Anger is a choice."

Her statement needled him. Choose to let go his anger? Not likely. Some days the familiar knot in his gut was the thing that best gave him his cop's edge. No, he didn't buy into Abbie's psychobabble. On this subject they were not going to reach agreement.

Before he gave in to the urge to crush it in his fist, he hung the delicate Santa on the tree and searched for a change of topic. "Heard from Janis?"

"No." Abbie eyed him curiously. "Any leads on the missing mother?"

"Nothing. The state lab couldn't come up with anything on the fingerprints. We've sent them to neighboring states. We'll more than likely turn to the Internet.''

Abbie noted Ben's change in demeanor. He'd arrived so endearingly self-conscious. For a moment, with his question about the possibility of her having children, it had looked as if he might open up. But then he'd retreated from her suggestion that we could choose our responses to life, if not life's course. He still harbored much pent-up anger. She could sense it, and she hovered between two options. To help him or to let him help himself. Her choice would depend on how she felt about him. Deep down.

She suspected she might still love him.

And for that reason she'd help him. With patience. With understanding.

And by reaching out.

''You have enough frustration in your job right now. I'm sorry I jumped all over you earlier,'' she offered. ''About towing my car. It *was* a neighborly gesture. And it did save me considerable trouble. Thank you.''

He stared at her, surprise in his gray-blue eyes. ''I don't want to run your life for you.''

''No.'' She smiled, far too conscious of his disarming regard. ''Heaven knows, Herbie's already trying to do that.''

He smiled. Well, one corner of his mouth twitched, and Abbie chose to see the lopsided action as a smile. The mood in the room lightened considerably.

''Herbie. Suki. Tabitha. Clucky,'' he said. ''Not to mention Margot, Garrett and Sully.''

''Are we talking about my life or yours?'' To avoid

those blue eyes, Abbie picked up several small spunglass snowflake ornaments and hung them on the tree.

"This town doesn't seem to recognize the difference," he muttered.

She wanted to ask him just how much and in what way it bothered him that they were thrown together, but his electrifying nearness in close quarters made her reticent.

"It's Baby and this unusual foster situation." Reaching for a box of ornaments, she tried to make her voice nonchalant. "People will talk until the next newsworthy incident blows into town."

"I don't care about people." He stayed her hand as she unwrapped tissue from a luminous treetop angel. "It's what we think that matters. I'm...sorry I came on so strong when you first got back to town. I didn't know what you'd been through."

"Apology accepted." Knowing the effort his apology cost him, she took strength from it and from his touch. She handed him the angel. "Would you like to do the honors?"

He backed away as if the simple offer had stung him. "Go ahead," he said, his voice gruff, his eyes suddenly shadowed. "It's your tree."

Not pressing the issue, she stood on tiptoe to secure the lovely antique ornament on the highest branch of the little live tree. "Do you believe in angels, Ben?"

"I can't say I've felt their presence."

"I have. Almost constantly. Especially the past eight years."

He scowled. "You say that after all you've been through?"

"Especially after all I've been through." She stood back to survey her handiwork. "I've been blessed."

"I see people every day complaining about far better hands they've been dealt than the one dumped on you," he replied with a catch in his words and blatant admiration in his eyes. "Your attitude amazes me."

She smiled at him, heartened they were talking about life without backing away. "Sometimes it amazes me."

His expression had softened considerably. "Do you know where a cop could get a good guardian angel?"

"Ah, you must keep your eyes open, because they tend to pop up in the most unlikely places."

He chuckled. He actually chuckled.

"What's so funny?"

"M & M Hardware advertises there's nothing they don't sell. Let's set Herbie to searching the shelves for angels. It'll keep him out of our hair."

She liked his attempt at humor, as obviously rusty as it was. "How about Margot? Shall we set her looking?"

"Nah. Her dragon breath would scorch the little critters' wings."

A lovely new feeling entered the room. One of camaraderie. Of two against the world. The sensation resonated of the past. Of a lost relationship so intense Abbie had wished to live in it forever. For a moment, in Lily Arrondise's parlor, time stood still and possibility surrounded the former lovers.

Abbie felt the blood rush to her cheeks. The silly tinsel garland crown she'd forgotten she was wearing slipped over one ear. "Well…" She tried to remove the bit of frivolity, but it had become caught in one of her barrettes. "Shall we see about hanging the excess ornaments around the room?"

"That's some halo." With the most curious look of longing in his eyes, Ben reached out to extricate the tinsel. When he'd freed it from the barrette, he set it back upon her head. "Do you suppose you're my unlikely angel?"

For a minute she stopped breathing. Heavens, but he looked as if he might gobble her up as if she were some Christmas sugar cookie. "I..." Words snagged in her throat as he pulled her into his arms.

His eyes told her this time he had no intention of warning her off.

He held her hard against him. Threaded his fingers through her hair. Positioned her head so that she had to look at him. Then, never taking his gaze from hers, he lowered his mouth to cover her lips with an excruciating deliberation. It was almost as if he were giving her every opportunity to back out, to protest, to break the spell.

Oh, sure. When flounders flew.

With the sensation of waves crashing against her heart, she flung her arms around his neck and claimed him. She was a fool to want him. She was a fool to resist him. It was said fools rush in where angels fear to tread. Eight years of restraint crumbled like a sand castle before the incoming tide. She gloried in his kiss.

His hot, probing kiss.

With a deep, guttural moan, he swept his tongue across her lips. She opened for him. Welcomed him. Felt the heat of his passion warm her in places she'd kept locked and protected for years. Emotional places. Physical places. Dangerous places.

She felt released from her self-imposed bondage. Released and reckless. And wanted.

He ran his hands down her back. Cupped her bottom. Made shivers run up her spine.

"Abbie." Her name escaped his lips, a ragged sigh. He kissed her neck. Her earlobe. Her eyelids.

Thrilling to the desire she'd suppressed for so long, she ran her hands over his chest. Marveled at the hard muscle surfaces, their warmth seeping through his shirt. Electrifying her hands.

He ran his lips, the tip of his tongue, over her cheekbone. Down her jaw. Along her chin.

Her knees threatened not to support her.

He claimed her with his hands, running his palms over her hips. Her waist. The sides of her breasts—

Her *breast*. And her prosthesis.

And under her prosthesis, her scar. Her badge of courage. Not, however, a badge of sexuality.

"Oh, no!" Panic caught her. Hauled her from the pinnacle of fantasy. She wasn't ready to test Ben. To test her womanhood. Herself. Her heart hammering in her throat, she pulled away. "I can't...I can't."

Fearing rejection, she rejected him in a preemptive strike.

"Abbie, what's wrong?" Holding on to her arms as if she might slip away and disappear for good, he stood before her, his chest heaving, his eyes still glazed with desire.

She tried to turn away from him, but he held her firm. "What's wrong?" he repeated.

"I don't know how to tell you." If he were a

stranger, she could explain. She could be brave. But he was Ben. And she'd once loved him and been loved in return. Physically. Oh, so physically. Who knew how much deeper their love went in his regard? Not knowing, she couldn't chance his pity. Or worse. His turning away.

"There's something been eating at you since you returned. I can sense it." He cupped her face between his enormous, weather-roughened hands. "You have to get it out in the open. I can't stand thinking I might get ambushed at any minute by answers to questions I never dreamed of asking."

His tenderness undid her. She struggled against tears. Slipped out of his grasp. Stood beyond his reach.

"Abbie…"

"I had breast cancer." She swallowed hard and drew on every calming mantra she'd ever uttered. "I had a mastectomy. I have one breast."

Instead of capturing her and holding her prisoner, the words liberated her. They were like a key to a cramped cell. She took courage from the open door, in the unexpected sense of freedom. "That's who I am now," she whispered, marshaling courage. "That's the new Abbie Latham."

She embraced her name as she would a lover. Even if she lost Ben, she must face the mirror every morning. She must accept and cherish who she was.

Ben could find no words to respond.

Against all good judgment, he stared at her. At her soft womanly curves. At the small firm breasts he'd caressed. She looked so perfect. He couldn't envision her otherwise.

Under his inappropriate scrutiny, she took a step backward, a look of—what? Warning?—on her face. He didn't blame her. He had no right to stare. He needed to say something. Anything. To offer up understanding. But what did you say to a survivor?

Her declaration left him dumbfounded. Reeling.

Yesterday, when she'd told him of her cancer, he'd thought of it in nonspecific terms. Horrifying, but vague. Now she'd put a body part to the horror. An amputation. A brutal loss. His gut roiled. Nausea rose in his throat at the thought of Abbie—his beautiful Abbie—being cut. Being violated. If there had been a way for him to take her place in her ordeal, to spare her, he would have jumped at the sacrifice.

"Ben?" Abbie gripped his arm. "Do you need to sit down?"

He needed to pull himself together. For her.

"Shall I get you a glass of water?"

"No." He managed to grind out the word.

"I'm sorry I coldcocked you." She released his arm, determination in her green eyes. "But you needed to know why I'm not ready—" Her hand fluttered to her shoulder, but she didn't seem to find what she was looking for. "I'm not ready for a relationship." She squared her shoulders, took a second step back.

Dammit, she was pushing him away, and he couldn't find the words to pull her back. "Abbie...I don't know what to say. Don't even know what to ask."

"It's a lot to digest. Perhaps you should sleep on it." She sighed and distanced herself with that long, slow exhalation.

He shook his head. In shock. "There are no more secrets?"

"No more secrets." She wrapped her arms around her chest in a protective embrace. She didn't look vulnerable, as he might have expected. She looked indomitable. Determined to shut him out one more time. "I'm tired, Ben. You'd better go."

He didn't want to, but she cloaked herself in a mantle of self-sufficiency. Left him in the cold. Again.

"I'll be back," he said, reaching for his coat.

"I'm not sure that would be wise." Her chin quivered. Clearly, she wanted him to leave.

As he picked up his jacket, his determination matched hers. He'd leave, but he'd be back. Hell, when had he ever been wise where Abbie Latham was concerned?

Chapter Ten

Monday morning Pat Spenser dropped by the cottage on her way to opening the library. She suggested Abbie could be very flexible in her training hours as long as she still cared for Baby. A doting grandmother herself, Pat seemed unflappable, faced with the prospect of an infant's presence in the library. Abbie promised she'd make it in after lunch when Baby would most likely take his nap in his car seat.

Janis dropped by on her way to work to say she hadn't found a more permanent foster home.

Clucky Tillman dropped off a still-frozen fruitcake and a load of gossip. She claimed the Chase siblings were publicly giving Ben a hard time regarding his association with Abbie. To extricate herself from Clucky, Abbie pleaded a desperate need to take advantage of Baby's morning nap to contact the utilities to transfer services to her name. When it was obvious she'd get no rise out of Abbie, Clucky left, muttering something about a "waste of good fruitcake."

The morning flew by in a blur of visitors, calls on her recharged cell phone and baby ministrations. Abbie barely had a moment to think of her latest encounter with Ben.

Just before noon, the weather broke and the sun came out. She seized the opportunity for a walk with Baby. As soon as the fresh air hit her face, the memory of last evening's events settled in her thoughts with alarming clarity.

Why had she pushed Ben away before he'd had a chance to fully absorb the fallout of her revelations? The evening had been young. Baby still slept. They'd had an opportunity to discuss the issue until no questions remained. Why, then, had she sent Ben home?

She knew the answer. The difficulty came in facing the truth.

Her breast cancer and her mastectomy weren't simply clinical issues now that Ben was on the scene. When he reentered her life, so, too, did the elements of rekindled desire and long-suppressed dreams for a future. With those ingredients, he turned her existence—her hard-won equilibrium—into a bubbling, emotional stew.

The truth-or-dare kicker seemed to be that she preferred this impassioned predicament to the cool, detached state she'd cultivated for so long.

So why had she sent Ben away?

Scowling with intense reflection, Abbie now plowed through snow on the Pier Road sidewalk, pulling Baby in his car-seat sled. "Pushing Ben away,

I must look like a chicken. A coward. A real wuss,'' she declared.

Baby gave her one of those if-you-say-so looks before jamming his snowsuit-encased fist in his mouth. Was he teething? Was she destined for teething on top of testosterone in her life?

She wanted to do the right thing by Baby. Not only did she keep his well-being uppermost in her mind, but his good-natured dependency had become almost like a fix. She wanted the high taking care of him gave her. She wanted the whiff of the future his presence promised.

And Ben.

What did she want from him?

More than she cared to admit.

She wanted him to understand why she'd felt she had to leave eight years ago. She wanted his forgiveness. She wanted his friendship—

"Liar. You want him."

The words descended upon her from out of nowhere. Baby certainly hadn't spoken. The pronouncement sounded so Murphy-esque that Abbie was shocked she'd actually been the one to speak it. Her slip of the tongue only proved she knew more about her inner self than was safe to confess.

How could she figure out what to do with Ben when her own true wants and needs were at war with her best interest? Uncorking Ben's bottled anger would surely put her peace of mind at risk. A renewed relationship with him was not a stop on her journey to serenity and well-being, was not why she'd returned to Point Narrows.

Want. Ah, there was the rub. At some time, when

she'd let down her guard, want had crept up behind her. Had disguised itself as need.

Was it want or need that put her on the Pier Road, heading straight for the government wharf at noon? Heading straight for The Shack, the take-out stand where most lobstermen, most utility and construction workers—most *cops*—for miles around ate their midday meal. She was sure to see at least one Chase.

In rounding the bend, she saw five.

Tobias. Garrett. Sully. Jonas. And Ben.

Standing around in the chill noonday sun, arguing animatedly over steaming chowder spooned from plastic containers. Abbie could tell from the family's body language alone that the conversation was weighted against Ben.

She didn't need to be a rocket scientist to deduce the source of their agitation. Ben's relationship with her.

Clucky's gossip came to mind, fueling Abbie's frustration. It was high time the gossip and speculation stopped, and she now had the opportunity to cut it off at its source.

Fairly quivering with determination, she pulled Baby's sled to a halt before the men. "Hello."

All but Ben mumbled an inarticulate response.

"How are you doing?" he asked. His eyes flickered with emotion. Empathy? Pain? Pity? What did he feel when he looked at her now? When he knew the truth of her situation.

"I'm fine." She screwed her courage to the sticking place and shot each man a piercing glance.

Sully returned her gaze with open hostility. Ben's father, Tobias, studied her with an off-putting dispassion as if his emotions had long ago booked out of town. Garrett narrowed his eyes, his expression unreadable. Only eighteen-year-old Jonas showed any eagerness at her appearance, but that eagerness seemed vaguely predatory.

Ben's gray-blue eyes flickered with wariness as his stance between Abbie and his family suggested he'd been caught in the middle.

As workers passed close by the small group, the air hung with explosive possibilities.

"You wouldn't happen to be talking about me, would you?" Abbie asked, deliberately igniting the fuse.

To their credit, the men couldn't hide their guilty-as-charged expressions.

"The only reason I asked," she continued, "is so that I could be party to the conversation. I mean, if I'm to be the subject, I should have the opportunity to present my side of the story. Right?"

"I gotta go," Sully muttered.

"No!" Abbie held out her hand. "Sully Chase, you wouldn't speak to me Saturday in the square. You won't speak to me now. Why is that?"

Sully looked around, clearly uncomfortable with the gathering lunchtime crowd composed chiefly of lobstermen, construction workers and utility service personnel. His peers.

He squinted. "A man's entitled to his opinion."

Abbie didn't back down. "And yours, concerning me, is?"

Sully shrugged. "I think my brother's a fool for getting involved with you again."

Ben shot his brother a warning glare. "Sully—"

"It's okay," Abbie intervened. "I want to hear what he has to say."

"You dumped him," Sully growled, jerking his head toward Ben. "Practically at the altar. Without a word. And then you waltz back into town as if it didn't matter. If a man has his pride, he doesn't take that kind of treatment."

Abbie turned to Ben. "Have you told them why I left?"

"It wasn't my place."

"Well, it's mine." She clung to the rope on Baby's sled as if it were a lifeline.

"You don't have to do this, Abbie." Ben gently grasped her arm above her elbow. "Not publicly."

She did have to do this. Publicly. Ignorance was her disease's ally. "What better way to set the record straight?"

Sully planted his feet. "This should be interesting."

In a move that startled Abbie, Ben scooped Baby out of his car seat, then stood and slipped his free arm around her shoulder. She should have taken comfort from his strength, but she couldn't help wondering if he saw her as too fragile for this confrontation.

She wasn't fragile. Not by a long shot.

"I left eight years ago," she said, "because I discovered I had cancer. Breast cancer. Even after the mastectomy, I thought I was going to die. I came back to Point Narrows because I didn't die. Because I want a second chance at life. It's as simple as that."

The four Chases standing before her flinched. Even some of the closer bystanders moved away from their small group, as if Abbie's announcement was somehow contagious.

"God, Abbie. You could have told us." Ben's father flung his disposable cup into a nearby trash can.

Hah. This from a man who'd clammed up, who'd shared no feelings, who'd showed no emotion except for too much drink after Sandra Chase left town, Abbie noted, but resisted the opportunity to point out the contradiction. This conversation was not about scoring points. It should be about fostering understanding.

"I could have, yes," she replied instead, amazed at the difficulty in publicly admitting as much. "I may have made a mistake leaving without explanation. I underestimated…many people. Eight years have taught me a lot. I'm sorry I hurt Ben. I've told him so."

"Abbie." Ben pulled her closer. "You don't have to—"

"I'm not finished." Abbie looked into the faces of Ben's father and brothers. "Having apologized to the person I hurt, I think my decision to return to Point Narrows really is nobody's business but *mine*. If Ben and I decide to explore a new relationship, that's *our* business." She cocked one eyebrow. "So I'm telling you four meddling gentlemen to *butt out.* I mean it. Any questions?"

To her surprise, Abbie saw a flicker of admiration in Sully's eyes. The other three Chase men backed off. Literally.

"Now, if you'll excuse me—" she lifted Baby out of Ben's arms "—I'm hungry."

When she turned to place Baby in his car seat sled,

she came face-to-face with Margot standing directly behind her, sporting a conspiratorial grin.

"You go, girl," Margot muttered as she brushed by in pursuit of the retreating Chase men. "Hey, Garrett! You owe me twenty bucks, and today I'm collecting."

Ben hadn't moved. "You might just have them all," he said, the corner of his mouth twitching. "The lot of them. They admire guts."

"It had to be said." Abbie tucked Baby's blanket about him. He seemed unfazed by the adults' little standoff. "Maybe they'll leave you alone."

"I can take care of myself." His words were gruff, but his eyes twinkled with the hint of appreciation.

"Me, too."

"But do you want to go it alone?" His expression became sober. "Just now, you kind of made it seem we might have a future. What do you think? Do we?"

"I don't know. It all depends on the people we've become. I do know there are no more secrets. The past is out in the open and…well, *past*." She took a deep breath, determined not to hide her feelings any longer. "Whatever relationship we develop won't be a copy of eight years ago. Won't be based on the old Ben or the old Abbie. I'm a changed woman. You're going to have to deal with that."

He scowled. "I don't think I've changed."

"Then you're definitely going to have to deal with that."

"What's wrong with remaining constant?"

"Some constants stand the test of time. Love. Understanding. Compassion. Others, like anger and resentment, bring nothing but pain to the bearer and those around him.''

''Do you think I'm still angry at you?''

''Not just at me, but at your mother.'' She wrapped the rope to Baby's sled around her fist. ''If you can't deal with that anger, if you can't get through to the other side of your resentment, we have no future. I can't love a man who can't forgive.''

Ben watched her walk away. Watched the determination in her stride. Watched the firm set of her head and shoulders.

He'd underestimated her.

She'd stood up to his family. And he'd stood beside her. She'd issued them a challenge to butt out of her—*their*—business. They'd backed down. And then he'd expected her to turn to him with open arms.

Hey, it happened in the movies.

Instead, she'd turned and issued a challenge to him. To forget the past. In essence, to clean up his act. To deal with his anger.

Hell, his anger was part of who he was. *She* was going to have to deal with *that*.

Perhaps she had a right to demand he forgive and forget where their past was concerned. But she had no right to tell him how to feel where his mother was concerned.

That was *his* business. Chase business. She needed to butt out there.

Ben felt a burning desire to talk with a man who kept daily counsel with an unforgiving anger. He had to talk to his father.

Tobias Chase lived with his son Garrett and his granddaughter Mariah. Ben didn't want an audience for this conversation, however, so he waited for his father at four-thirty later that afternoon on Tobias's construction site, the Pennyman property.

"Pop!" Ben stepped out of his patrol car as his father emerged from the half-finished house.

"What's wrong?"

"I need to talk to you."

"Can we do it where it's warm? At home." Tobias moved toward his pickup. "Over a beer."

"No." Ben needed his father sober. "I don't want Garrett putting his two cents in."

Tobias stared hard at Ben. "It's Abbie, isn't it?"

"Yeah."

As if it were the last thing in the world he wanted to do, Tobias flung his toolbox into the back of his pickup, then slowly walked the distance to the cruiser. Without a word, he opened the passenger door and got in.

Before his father could change his mind, Ben, too, got into the car, sank into the familiar scent of wool and wood shavings. The scent he remembered from his childhood. Before his mother left. Before the alcohol.

"Well?" Tobias stared at him.

Ben struggled for a starting point, knowing full well this conversation wasn't going to be easy. He wanted to talk about Abbie, yes. Wanted to talk about the battle of conflicting desires that raged within him. Wanted guidance from a man who'd been through that war. But he was wary of seeking counsel from his father. Tobias Chase had never shared his own inner struggle. His children had seen the alcohol as a sign they shouldn't ask. By tacit agreement, Sandra Chase's name—as wife or mother—had always been off-limits.

"Abbie...she still means a lot to me," Ben said at last.

"Does she feel the same way about you?"

Ben stared at his father, surprised at his question, unsettled by the fact Tobias hadn't immediately repudiated Abbie, as the rest of the family had done.

"Does she?" Tobias repeated.

This was no time for hedging. "I think she wants to."

"What the hell does that mean?"

"She kissed me as if she does. But she told me she couldn't love a man who wouldn't let go of the past. Of his anger. Couldn't love a man who wouldn't forgive. She mentioned herself and...Mom." The last word was one of the hardest he'd ever had to speak.

Ben waited for Tobias's angry reaction. He had no illusions his father was too old to take him on. Physically, if necessary. He'd charged into forbidden territory. He deserved what he got.

What he got was an unnerving silence.

Tobias sat stone still. He stared through the cruiser windshield, his gaze flinty, his jaw muscle twitching. "So she wants you to change," he said finally, the words raw and filled with pain.

"Yeah." Ben felt solidarity with his father's resistance.

"After an eight-year, unexplained absence, she reappears with an apology and wants to erase your anger. Your well-deserved anger." Tobias fisted his hands in his lap. "Forgive and forget, she wants."

"Yes." Ben's stomach knotted. "That's a lot to ask a man. As much as I want her—"

"She's right, dammit."

Ben couldn't believe his ears. "Pop?"

"Son—" his weathered cheeks splotched with crimson, Tobias turned to face Ben "—I'm going to give you an early Christmas present. A confession."

Ben sucked in air as if he were suffocating.

"Do you remember what your mother wrote the day she left?"

Remember? He'd forgotten nothing about that day. December seventh. Pearl Harbor day. Sandra Chase must not have thought the date got enough attention. She had to drop her own bomb.

On the fat-lined notebook paper Ben had pried out of his father's hand, his mother had written, "You've worn me out. I'm leaving before I hurt myself or you or both of us."

He should have known, by the use of *both,* that she'd been talking to Pop, but from where Ben had stood, at twelve, it had seemed she'd been accusing the kids, too.

"I remember," he replied, his senses pinched with the memory.

"She was right. I did wear her out. With my attitude." Tobias's strong hands trembled. "And hell would freeze over before I'd change."

"How did you wear her out? I don't understand." Ben searched his childhood recollections from the standpoint of a cop, trying to come up with spousal abuse or neglect. He couldn't find any. "You worked hard. You put food on the table. You made sure we kids helped out around the house, respected her. *You* respected her.''

''No. I didn't respect her. Not the way she needed respect.''

''What are you talking about?'' He'd never seen his father speak an offensive word to his mother, never seen him lift a hand against her. ''What could you have done different?''

''I could have let her be herself.''

Ben's mind reeled with his father's revelation. ''How so?''

''Your mother was a talented woman. She played piano. Sang. In a fancy hotel in Boston. I met her when I did my stint in the navy.''

Ben had never heard his mother sing. Ever. Not even lullabies. They'd never had a piano in the house.

''When she married me, I told her things would have to change. I'd take care of her. A good man takes care of his woman. As my father had my mother. As my grandfather had my grandmother. She had to understand she'd married a proud man.''

''What's wrong with that?''

''You know what they say about pride.'' Tobias's shrug seemed more like a painful wince.

''But she married you, knowing the kind of man you were.''

''Oh, she loved me. Love is blind at the beginning. When you're both hot and bothered. When you'll promise anything.''

Ben had never thought of his parents in those terms. When he was twelve, he saw them in the light of his own needs. As security. As a unit. They weren't particularly demonstrative or affectionate toward each other, but they weren't all that different from his friends' parents. They were good parents. That's what he recalled. He'd never bothered to wonder whether they were good as husband and wife.

"What happened?" he asked.

"I wouldn't let her work. Put my foot down. Especially after you kids came along."

"The construction business was booming around here." Ben felt a compulsion to rationalize his father's decision. "We never went without."

"She went without. Inside."

"What could she have done? This is Point Narrows, not Boston."

"Piano bar in the summer hotels, maybe. Lessons in the winter. She said she didn't care. Said she needed an outlet for self-expression. Said she felt like half a woman."

"She had us."

"She loved you, but she needed more."

"Yeah." Ben snorted in disgust. "So she left us."

Tobias sighed wearily. "I think she felt so trapped, she was afraid she'd do something rash. She knew I'd take care of you kids. Knew she might not be able to afford to. So she left you with me. Maybe she saw leaving as a way to protect you. From her."

"She hurt us to spare us. I've heard that one before." An old bitter feeling of abandonment washed over Ben. "Well, I don't buy it."

"Son." Tobias laid his work-roughened hand on Ben's arm. "Do I look like a happy man?"

Ben was startled into silence. The Chase men rarely touched and even more infrequently bared their feelings.

"Do I look as if my stubbornness, my unwillingness to give an inch has brought me one ounce of good?" Tobias persisted as if he'd seized a cause. "What I'm trying to tell you—warn you—is not to bring on unnecessary heartache."

"You did what you thought was right, Pop."

"So did your mother. I forced her into a corner."

"Are you telling me you'd do it differently?"

"If your mother walked back into town...in a heartbeat."

Shock rippled through Ben. Throughout the years he'd thought anger had driven his father to drink, while all along it had been sorrow.

"After what she did, you still love her?" He asked the question not as a son asking his father, but as a man would ask another man.

Tobias shifted on the seat. Pulled his wallet from his back pocket. Opened it. Pushed aside bills. Lifted a flap. And from a hidden place he removed an old photo of a woman smiling at the camera as if her world overflowed with love and happiness. Ben's mother.

"I always carry it with me," Tobias said, running his thumb over the dulled image.

"I never knew." Ben thought of the house in which he'd grown up. A house devoid of any trace of his mother.

"Abbie didn't tell you?"

"How would she have known?"

"Looking for you, she came upon me once. Just after you'd started dating. I was sitting in the kitchen all alone. Looking at this picture." Tobias's eyes glittered. "I asked her to promise she wouldn't tell any of you kids I had it."

"Why the hell not?"

"I didn't want to hurt you." He smoothed a finger over his wife in the photo as if he were caressing her. "Looking back on it, maybe I was selfish. I'm sorry."

So many secrets. So much pain. What would it take for people to be honest with each other?

"Don't be hard on Abbie," Tobias urged. "*She* came back."

Ben clutched the patrol car's steering wheel until his fingers threatened to go numb. His mother was still wrong, dammit. For all his father's misgivings. If you cared about people, you didn't throw them away. He thought about his mother. He thought about Abbie. He thought about Baby's mother. His thoughts made his blood boil.

"Anger will kill you, son."

Ben didn't need his father to tell him that. His anger was eating him from the inside out. But, having nurtured it for years, he didn't know how to begin to let it go.

Chapter Eleven

The library's final patron of the afternoon, six-year-old Mariah Chase, stood before the checkout desk and, with tongue licking the corner of her mouth, painstakingly signed the cards for a stack of books she and Abbie had just chosen. The child was an avid reader, precociously opinionated when it came to her reading tastes, and a librarian's joy to assist. Helping her had made Abbie's afternoon.

In fact, the entire day's activities, including putting the Chase men in their place earlier, had been remarkably satisfying. Perhaps poor old Mondays had been given a bad rap.

"How long do you think it will take to read all these books?" Abbie asked Mariah.

The little girl squinched her face in thought. "A

week. Unless there's a really good one. Then it takes longer.''

''Because you don't want it to end?''

''No. Because I have to read it twice. Once for me. Then again with Daddy. After the TV news.''

Abbie beamed with delight. ''You read to your daddy?''

''Only the adventure stuff. And mysteries. He won't let me read him the animal stories. They always make him cry.''

With a chuckle, Abbie mentally filed away that fact on the very macho Mr. Garrett Chase as she filed the charge cards from Mariah's selections.

Garrett's daughter loaded her books into a back-pack. ''See you next week.''

''Oh, Mariah?'' Pat Spenser, who was rocking Baby over in the story corner, called out. ''Have you given any thought to joining the Little Gulls? My daughter's getting the troop roster ready. The sign-up sheet's right on the desk.''

Mariah's sweet little mouth turned down. ''I don't think so,'' she mumbled, then scurried from the library without a backward glance.

''What was that all about?'' Abbie asked, walking to the door to flip the Open sign to Closed.

''My daughter and her friends are starting a girl's scouting group, divided according to age. The nature and wilderness skills would be geared to the seacoast, but all the other activities aim to create a sense of self-esteem and sisterhood. Just the way those national groups do.'' Pat sighed as she stroked Baby's head. ''I think Mariah needs a group like that.''

''Why Mariah, specifically?'' Abbie hadn't picked

up on any lack in the little girl's life. "I know she doesn't have a sister, but she has two girl cousins."

Pat raised her eyebrows. "She has no mother."

"But she seems to have an involved father. You heard her say they read together."

"That girl could use a woman's touch."

"Whatever do you mean? She seems bright. Motivated. Happy."

"I know this sounds shallow, but—" Pat took a deep breath "—did you see her clothes? Her hair? Garrett makes good money as a lobsterman. He could afford to take her shopping somewhere other than the church thrift shop and that sportsman's outlet. A pretty bow now and again certainly wouldn't hurt."

Abbie had noted nothing more than a six-year-old's mismatched play clothes, and an active child's tousled hair.

"Little girls can be very cruel to those who are different," Pat continued, "and Mariah isn't very…well, feminine. Garrett cuts her hair himself, you know. A bowl cut. Just the way Ben used to cut his."

Abbie couldn't believe her ears. "Is this a problem? If it is, I think the problem rests with the other little girls and their parents—"

"I'm only saying Mariah would benefit from interacting with those other little girls. And their mothers. She might pick up a little refinement, a sense of fashion, some social graces. Heaven knows Garrett—men in general—are clueless on such matters."

"Then I'm clueless, too," Abbie declared.

"That's because you're not a mother, dear." Pat forged on, unaware of her thoughtless observation.

"But you do know Garrett. And now Mariah. Perhaps you could speak to him. Urge him to enroll his daughter in the Little Gulls."

"I think that's up to Mariah." Abbie began gathering Baby's things. She hadn't seen any evidence that Mariah was neglected or unhappy. Moreover, after having told Garrett to butt out of her business earlier today, she didn't think he'd welcome her butting in to his. "Mariah seems content with her books."

"Isolation will not help that child."

"If she does indeed need help," Abbie replied, taking Baby from Pat, "a few hair bows and a new matching outfit won't cut it."

"I'm talking about fitting in, Abbie. About acceptance."

Pat couldn't know what a hot button that was. She might be misguided in her assessment of the causes, but she was right to be worried about an individual on the cusp of rejection.

"I'll watch the situation," Abbie conceded. "Perhaps I'll run it by Ben."

"Thank you." Pat tickled Baby's nose as Abbie bundled him in his snowsuit. "Mariah's a dear little girl, just as Baby's a dear little boy. I don't want either one to feel left out."

Neither did Abbie. She knew far too well what it felt like to stand on the outside looking in. But she'd wanted to remain cool and detached in returning to Point Narrows. For her own personal well-being. Increasingly, she found her detachment beginning to melt like icicles in a January thaw as she became involved in the community, in the well-being of others.

As she lifted Baby to place him in his car seat, he reached out and snagged a lock of her hair. Hanging on tightly, he cooed with obvious delight.

"Well, now! That's the first time you've performed that trick." She extricated her hair, then nuzzled Baby's chubby hand. "And you look pretty proud of yourself for it." Her own heart swelled with a sense of pride at his accomplishment.

"From now on, it'll be a new trick a day," Pat declared. "Just watch."

"I can't wait." Even as anticipation flooded her with happiness, Abbie felt a tiny niggling prick of dread. For the day when Baby would leave her.

She needed to talk to Janis, to deal with her conflicting feelings. Better still, she needed to talk to Ben. Janis had said he'd fostered a child only once because he'd found letting go extremely difficult. He'd understand her dilemma now.

"I'll see you tomorrow morning," she said to Pat. "Baby has a well-child checkup in the afternoon."

"Call first." Pat angled a glance out the window. "They're predicting snow and lots of it. We're a small operation. We close if it's too dangerous for staff or patrons to make it in."

"I'll call."

Shouldering Baby's infant bag and cradling him in his car seat, Abbie made her way to her car as Pat held doors open.

"You're getting good at this," Pat commented in parting.

Too good, Abbie thought as she drove home under dark, threatening skies. She had to remind herself she was Baby's foster mom, not his biological—nor even

his adoptive—mother. Having accepted imperma-
nence in her life—an even, day-to-day progression—
she didn't need to cultivate a craving for tenure.

As she pulled into her cottage's drive, a gust of
wind drove sleety flakes off the harbor. Much more
of that and the roads would be dangerously slick. Abbie hustled Baby into the house. She loved the pic-
ture-perfect white of a snowfall, but she hadn't forgotten the variety of messy precipitation the coastline
could provide. She was out of practice traveling on
icy roads.

"Murphy," she declared, fingering the little gold
pin on her coat lapel, "I'm putting you on overtime.
I now have Baby to think of, and a job. And my
parents' flight in four days."

Goodness, her parents would be flying in this wintry weather, and she hadn't even turned on the tele-
vision or the radio since she'd arrived in Point Narrows. Had the airports been operating smoothly?
What was brewing out over the ocean? What was
forecast for the day before Christmas?

Ben would know. She needed to talk to Ben.

Placing Baby in his car seat on the kitchen table,
she drew herself up short. How many times this afternoon had she reminded herself she must speak with
Ben? As if he'd become an integral part of her daily
decision-making process, of her new life in Point Narrows.

Baby answered her with a hungry yowl.

Shrugging out of her coat to prepare a bottle of
formula, Abbie thought how she hadn't even given
Ben an opportunity to discuss her mastectomy. Although this morning at the pier, he'd seemed as at

ease in her presence as one would expect him to be while she took on his family. He'd even seemed protective. Now, that unnerved her somewhat. Was he protective because he had deep feelings for her, or was he protective because he saw her as weak? Disabled.

They needed to talk.

She'd invite him to supper one night this week. Just him and her and Baby. The thought infused her heart with a lovely warm sensation.

As she settled with Baby and bottle in the rocker by the stove, she managed to dig her cell phone out of her pocket. Managed to punch in the number for the police station.

"See, Baby," she cooed as she waited for a response, "thanks to you, I'm now capable of multitasking! You're not the only one learning new tricks."

"Point Narrows Communications Center."

"Chief Chase, please."

"The chief has gone to Portsmouth on a case."

Abbie's spirits sagged. "Do you know when he'll be back?"

"It's open-ended."

"Oh, my." Abbie sighed. And he hadn't even told her.

"Any message?"

"No. Thank you. I'll get in touch when he gets back." As she hung up, she cuddled Baby closer to her. The wind howled outside. Suddenly Point Narrows seemed bleaker without Ben's presence.

He'd spent three days on a wild-goose chase, from Portsmouth to Boston to Portsmouth again, and every step of the way he'd thought of Abbie. It wasn't as if thoughts of her interfered with his investigation. On the contrary, it was as if her felt presence enhanced his work. As he followed the leads, as he questioned tipsters, he felt her compassion, and that sense of empathy enabled him to walk in another's shoes, enabled him to question and listen on a different level.

His questioning had been for naught, however. The tips hadn't panned out. Not even this last one on the return trip to Portsmouth. The trail grew cold. Baby's mother remained missing.

Standing near the vending machines at police headquarters, Ben wrapped his hands around a cup of coffee and contemplated the drive back to Point Narrows. He needed to talk to Abbie. About this fruitless investigation. About his father's revelation. About her mastectomy. About them.

"Chase! Glad you didn't leave." Sergeant Mark Reuters, Ben's contact in Portsmouth, approached. "We just brought in someone you might want to question."

"What's the background?"

"We got called to the scene of a domestic dispute. When we arrived, the woman was bruised pretty bad, but she didn't want to press charges on the boyfriend."

"Peace on earth, goodwill toward men," Ben grunted. It was hard not to sink into cynicism. Harder still not to personalize these all-too-routine police encounters, not to see his sister's—or Abbie's—face on the women involved. "Where do I come in?"

"The boyfriend seemed far too cocky. Far too sure

she wouldn't blow him in. He kept taunting her. 'Remember the baby,' he kept saying. And here they're living together, unmarried. No kids.'' Reuters narrowed his eyes in disgust. "Whatever he meant by the warning, it seemed strong enough to shut the girlfriend up. The responding officer remembered your investigation and brought her in for questioning.''

Ben threw his coffee cup in the trash. "Let's do it.''

Reuters ushered him into a room where a young woman, scarcely over twenty by the look of her, sat at the end of a long table. She looked up with fear in her eyes. Or eye. Purple swelling closed her right eye.

What kind of a world-turned-upside-down made her fear the police who'd rescued her from a boyfriend who'd abused her? If she was Baby's missing mother, she was one hurting soul. She couldn't take care of herself, let alone an infant. Ben swallowed the bitter bile rising in his throat. To get answers, he'd have to trade on her vulnerability, and that hard reality made him feel less a man.

Damn. Was he losing his cop's edge?

"I'll leave you two.'' Reuters closed the door behind him.

"You want something to drink?'' Ben asked the woman. "Coffee? A cola?''

She shook her head, but didn't speak. In fact, she looked down, as if ashamed of her appearance. She was the victim, dammit, and *she* felt shame. He wanted to punch the absent boyfriend through a wall.

Halfway down the table, Ben sat on the edge and read the responding officer's report. The young woman's name was Jenni. He tried to think less how

Reuters might get answers, more how Abbie might. "Jenni, I can get you into a shelter," he said.

Without looking up, Jenni shook her head.

"He could kill you if you go back."

Snuffling, she mumbled something that on first hearing sounded like, "If I don't go back, he'll kill me."

On second thought, it sounded like, "If I don't go back, he'll tell on me."

Ben played the hunch. "Tell what, Jenni?"

She flinched. Fat teardrops fell on her rumpled sweatshirt front. Whatever secret she held inside, she was tired of lugging it around. Tired of it holding her hostage.

Personally, he'd had it up to here with secrets. They did nothing but undermine your chances of living clean and free.

"Jenni, is this secret about your boyfriend? 'Cause he's not the kind of guy worth protecting."

She shook her head and rubbed the sleeve of her sweatshirt across her nose.

He dug into his pocket for an unused handkerchief. Handed it to her. Waited and tried not to show his impatience. Not with her. With the jerk she might be protecting.

"Did he do something to your baby?"

Burying her face in the handkerchief, she convulsed in sobs.

"Tell me about the baby, Jenni." He tried to suppress thoughts of the child for a moment, tried to see this girl-woman as his sister. Tried to focus on how he could help her by getting her to confess whatever awful secret she harbored. The technique of personalizing an investigation took him into dangerous territory. Took him beyond standard police work and into the realm of a painful humanity.

"He…he…he didn't…want me to…keep him," she hiccuped.

"Your boyfriend didn't want you to keep your baby?"

Her face hidden, she bobbed her head in assent.

"What did he do?" Ben steeled himself for the answer. If Baby was Jenni's son, he was home with Abbie. Safe and sound. And loved. If Baby wasn't her son, dear Lord, Ben had been down this sorry road too many times and had hated every step of the way.

"What did your boyfriend do?" he repeated, this time more forcefully.

"He…made me…give him up."

"Give him up? Are we talking abortion, Jenni?"

Her face still plunged in the handkerchief, she shook her head vigorously.

"Did you leave him somewhere?"

"No!" She raised her head, outrage on her face. *"I loved him."*

"Where is he now, Jenni?" Ben abandoned his standing position of authority. Chucking procedure, he pulled a chair up to the table, far enough away from the young woman so as not to seem intimidating, but close enough to seem human. "Where's your baby?"

"With…with my cousin." She blew her nose loudly. "In New York. Last year."

Ben hadn't expected this. "Your cousin adopted your baby?"

Jenni lowered her head again. "You could say that."

"But if you said that, your boyfriend would have no reason to blackmail you." He willed the desperate young woman to look at him. "What really happened?"

Silent sobs shook her shoulders.

"Get it out, Jenni. Holding on to it is going to drag you down. You'll feel so low you won't recognize yourself."

"How much lower can I feel?" she wailed.

"Low enough to go back to that homicidal creep of a boyfriend," he growled.

Jenni turned a horrified face on Ben. "We needed the money." She ground out the words. "My folks cut me off."

"You sold your baby." The bottom dropped out of his heart.

"He's with my cousin. Family. Good people," she sobbed. "I couldn't keep him. I was afraid Derek would…hurt him."

For whatever reasons, she'd sold her child.

Ben knew what he had to do as a lawman. But a voice, a voice that sounded uncannily like Abbie's, urged him to do something as a human being.

"I'm going to get you to a safe shelter," he said, swallowing that old rising anger.

"But Derek—"

"Can't touch you now that you've told me everything." He looked hard at Jenni. "You have told me everything?"

Tears streaming down her cheeks, she looked right back at him. Nodded.

"Do you understand the consequences for selling a baby?"

"Yes." She appeared as if every ounce of hope had drained from her. "Far more than you'd ever imagine."

"This is what I'm going to do." Ben pinched the bridge of his nose. He'd never colored so far outside the lines. "I'm going to find your cousin in New York. If your baby's okay, we'll engineer a legal adoption." He glared at Jenni. "If he's not, I'm coming after you."

"Thank you," she sobbed. Reaching across the table, she clutched his hand. The look of relief on her face said she truly believed he'd find her son well cared for. Truly believed she had, in the worst possible way, done the right thing.

He rose and left the room, amazed to discover that in the midst of Jenni's sad, tawdry mess a small chunk of his own anger had broken free from the viselike grip it held on his heart. He felt less a police officer, but more a man.

The only regret he had was that he'd come no closer to finding Baby's mother.

She felt as if she were burning up, but didn't remember having stoked the fire. Throwing the covers off, she sat up and immediately succumbed to nausea. Hanging on to the edge of the bed, she dry heaved. She couldn't remember the last time she'd eaten. When the wave of nausea passed, she flopped back on the cot. Or thought she did. She wound up on her hands and knees on the rough floor. She couldn't find the strength to stand up. It hurt to breathe.

"Justin," she whimpered aloud. "I'm sorry."

A loud banging shook the air around her. Made her want to crawl inside her skin and hide. She flopped on her side on the floor. The room spun.

"Heather!" A girl's voice. "Heather, open up, dammit!"

She could see a girl and a boy at the window. She didn't recognize them. She wasn't about to open up to strangers. To shut them out, she pulled herself partway under the cot. Hid. Began to cry.

"We can see you, Heather! You're scaring us! Open up!"

Who was Heather?

Her chin on the splintery floorboards, she covered her ears with her hands. Her hair felt as if it were on fire. Where the hell was she?

Hell. Yeah.

"I'll break down the door." The boy's voice.

"Zeke, my parents would kill me."

"She's freakin' sick! We gotta do something."

"Oh, my God, my parents!" the girl shrieked. "Heather! Hang in there! I'll bring my parents."

Her parents.

No, she mouthed. Her parents would be so disappointed. She'd screwed up. Bad. She'd let them down. Let Justin down.

But as much as she'd let him down, she held on to the thought of Justin. If she let go, she might go under.

Chapter Twelve

December twenty-third and still no sign of Ben. Three days he'd been gone, with no word. Abbie had called the police station every day, only to be told he was still on a case, first in Portsmouth, then in Boston.

She missed him.

With growing concern for incoming stormy weather and for Ben on slick roads, she gazed out the library window. Although the church clock had just struck three, clouds had shrouded the afternoon in darkness, making the streetlights flicker on. Snow had begun to fall in earnest.

More than just missing Ben, Abbie realized how painful it was to be left behind without explanation.

She turned to the only other people in the library, a teenage boy named Myron, who slept noisily, his head pillowed on a table with his high school letter jacket, and a teenage girl named Brynna, who played with Baby.

Pat Spenser had left early to spend the holiday with her children down east, leaving Abbie in charge today and tomorrow.

"If the snow gets any worse," Abbie said to Brynna, "I'm going to close early."

"I'd close early. Like now."

Ben!

Abbie spun around to feast her eyes on his snow-flaked figure looming large in the doorway. She'd never been so glad to see anyone in her life. Because of the two teenagers in the room, she suppressed the impulse to throw herself into his arms.

Call her crazy, but he seemed glad to see her, too.

Although fatigue lines shadowed his eyes, their gray-blue depths showed an eagerness that fired her own excitement. He was unshaven, but his generous mouth curved in a smile. Not that sardonic twitch. No. He gifted her with a genuine, flash-of-strong-white-teeth grin. Abbie's pulse raced in reaction.

"So how have you and Baby been?" As he moved toward Brynna and Baby, his gaze lingered appreciatively on Abbie.

"F-fine," she stammered, suddenly schoolgirl shy.

He scooped Baby out of Brynna's arms as if he were the father. As if he were coming home. Baby answered him with a profusion of spit bubbles. "Hey, big guy! Where'd you learn that trick?"

"Oh, he's full of new tricks." With pride, Abbie stepped to Ben's side.

"I missed you!" Ben exclaimed, holding Baby high to nuzzle his stomach. "Ow!"

Baby had responded with his first new trick, well practiced now. He'd seized sizable hanks of Ben's dark hair in both his chubby fists. He now hung on for dear life.

Chuckling, Abbie disentangled Ben and secretly relished both the feel of Baby's tender flesh and Ben's thick hair. The heat from his scalp. The scent of the outdoors he'd brought into the library. His presence.

Oh, his remarkable presence.

Her heartbeat tap-danced for joy.

Brynna angled a glance from Baby to Ben to Abbie. "You're lucky you have short hair, Chief. I swear he's out to get Miss Latham and me!" With a bemused expression on her young face, Brynna retreated to the poetry section and pulled a book at random from the shelves. In a dramatic gesture, she turned her back to the adults.

"Did you discover anything about Baby's mother in Portsmouth or Boston?" Abbie asked in a hushed tone. Her intense curiosity turned immediately to embarrassment when she remembered Ben hadn't given her his itinerary. She'd just let slip she'd been keeping tabs on him.

The interest in his eyes and the quirk of his mouth revealed he acknowledged that slip. For a fleeting moment they stood in a private world where it was okay to care about the other's whereabouts and well-being. An electric anticipation arced between them. Something had changed in the three days they'd been apart. Changed for the good.

"Sorry," he said at last, his expression returning to sober. "No luck with the investigation. Just a bunch of false leads."

"Oh, dear." She wanted Baby reunited with his mother, certainly. For Baby's sake. But that didn't stop her from feeling a secret joy at the thought of having him as her own through the holiday. For her own sake. My, but she needed to discuss her conflicted emotions with someone who'd been in her situation.

"Could we talk sometime soon?" she asked. "About Baby, of course."

He didn't retreat as she thought he might. Instead, he looked her full in the face, captured her with his intense gaze. "We do need to talk. About Baby…and several other matters."

"When?"

"How about tonight? As soon as you've closed the library. As soon as I get cleaned up." He ran his free hand over his stubbled chin.

He didn't need to clean up for her. He looked perfect just as he stood before her. A little untamed. A lot sexy.

"I wouldn't want to give Baby a brush burn," he added.

Ah, Baby. Of course. How silly. She knew Ben had no need to spruce up for her.

"I'll cook," she offered.

"I'll bring Chinese," he countered. "Still like anything hot and spicy?"

"Oh, yes." She felt a little breathless at the prospect of hot and spicy with Ben. During their long courtship, they'd joked that Szechuan food was nectar of the gods. The love gods.

"Six o'clock okay?"

"It's a date," she replied without thinking, then blushed at the implications.

"Fine." He spoke the word with conviction, as if a date was just what he had in mind.

When he handed her Baby, she caught a glimpse of the three of them in the window's reflection. The image stole her heart away. Man. Woman. Child. It was all she'd ever wished for from the moment she'd started dating Ben. Before she'd made that fateful decision to exclude him from her life.

Ben and she definitely needed to talk. She needed to determine if they had a second chance. Against all sensible reasoning, she wanted an opportunity to reconcile, and no longer shied away from admitting it to herself. Perhaps she'd stiffen her backbone and confess as much to Ben. His absence and her yearning during that absence had made her bolder.

During the past three days she'd filled her waking hours with Baby and the library and settling into Miss Lily's cottage, and had discovered she needed more. She needed Ben. She wanted to expand her life to include him.

"I'll see you at six, then," she said with determination. "Bring chopsticks."

"Did I ever fail to?"

"Never," she breathed into the down on Baby's head. With a mixture of panic and pulse-racing anticipation she watched Ben leave.

"Miss Latham!" Brynna called out in a stage whisper as she stood at the wall stacks, ostensibly reading a book—except she held it upside down.

"Yes?" Ah, for a reference question to take her mind off Ben Chase.

"You and Chief Chase have a thing going?"

So much for that reference question.

"Thing?" Abbie blinked hard at the teenager's utter lack of guile.

"Yeah. Are you going out? Or dating. Or whatever adults call it." The girl lisped slightly in an effort to form words around her tongue stud. Kids today had so many holes in their bodies that Abbie wondered if they whistled in a stiff northeast breeze.

"We used to. A very long time ago," she replied, trying desperately not to blush. Again.

"What about now?"

"Mmmmm…now…I'm not sure." The blush won out.

Brynna followed Abbie as she made her way back to Baby's car seat on the charge desk.

"You could have him back if you wanted," Brynna persisted in a lispy whisper. "I saw the way he looked at you."

"You have an overactive imagination." Abbie sighed deeply at the thought of discussing her love life—or the lack thereof—with this teenager. "Besides, I've only been back in town a week. I'm still looking for a can opener in my furnished house, not romance."

Liar.

"Well, in case you ever are…" The young woman handed Abbie a business card.

The purple script proclaimed "Brynna Farley—Matchmaker. Employing only the best New Age technology."

Suppressing a grin, Abbie turned the card over in her fingers. "How old are you?

"Seventeen. But my gran says I have an ancient soul."

"How so?"

"I've always been able to identify with people of all ages. Different ways of thinking, too." Brynna pointed to the pin on Abbie's coat draped over the back of the chair. "Take that little gold angel you wear. A guardian angel, right?"

Having secured Baby in his car seat, Abbie reached out to touch her talisman. "Right," she answered softly.

"Well, some kids my age would think that's geeky. But I understand." The young woman pulled a crystal on a cord from the depths of her flannel shirt. "Good luck charms are cool. I can feel the need. We can all use a little help. Like my matchmaking."

"Have you had much success with this matchmaking business?" Abbie whispered as if they were dealing in illicit goods, as if a member of the board of trustees might walk in any minute and bust them. The girl's entrepreneurial spirit fascinated her, despite the fact that this conversation really didn't fall into any category of legitimate library activity.

"Success?" Brynna studied Abbie. "With kids, sure. But I'm looking to branch out with adults. I'll be graduating high school this year. I need to broaden my horizons. Take a shot at the real world, as my old man says."

"Your father?"

"No. Myron." Brynna stabbed a thumb in the direction of the jock snoring away, his head buried in his arms on the cluttered table. "My old man. My...boyfriend."

"So, you think you could fix me up with someone like Myron?" The thought threatened to make Abbie break out in giggles.

"Hey, I figure Chief Chase is as close as you're gonna get to my studmuffin."

So they'd come back to Ben Chase. Chief Studmuffin.

"I'll keep that in mind." Abbie slipped Brynna's card into the pocket of her slacks.

"Don't lose that." Brynna shoveled lank strands of hair out of her face. "I'm good and you're pretty. With that hair, it'd be easy to fix you up. Guys like long hair."

"Thank you. I think." In a self-conscious gesture, Abbie touched the velvet ribbon at the nape of her neck. The ribbon barely controlled the chestnut waves that tumbled halfway down her back.

"It's strange to see a woman your age who hasn't cut her hair." Brynna shrugged. "But cool," she added. "Definitely cool."

Myron awoke with a snort. "Hey, babe, you ready? I'm outa here."

"Sure!" Brynna spared a wink for Abbie. "You keep that card."

"I will." Abbie felt strangely touched by Brynna's concern, no matter the New Age Junior Achievement implications.

Perhaps the teenager did indeed have an old soul. In a most uncanny way Brynna had honed in on two outward symbols of Abbie's inner determination—her little gold guardian angel, Murphy, and her unfashionably long hair.

Murphy reminded her daily that, in her brush with

death eight years ago, she'd actually been very lucky. And her unshorn hair…well, that was a little treat to herself, a little feminine vanity after the ravages of chemo.

It was more than a treat. She shook her head and her hair and thought of how Ben had looked at her just now. Her long hair made her feel sexy. There, she'd said it, a four-letter word that had found little use in her vocabulary lately. Well, if the shoe fit… And if she felt sexy on the outside, couldn't she feel sexy straight through to the inside? With an impish grin, she swung her coat over her shoulders. She might have only one breast, but she did have great hair.

"Bye, Miss Latham!" Brynna called on her way out of the library with Myron. New Age Brynna, tall and willowy, was a half-head taller than her built-for-wrestling studmuffin.

Just outside the library windows, the two teenagers tangled limbs in a sloppy, uninhibited embrace.

Abbie smiled. Love was blind. If she were Cupid, she'd no more have thought to put those two together. Forget temperament. They were mismatched by looks alone. But when did chemistry pay any attention to looks alone?

She felt that little lesson tingle right down her mastectomy scar line. Long before Murphy, her mother had preached beauty was all in the eye of the beholder. Bless Mom, but that was easy to say for a woman with two breasts and a loving husband.

How did Ben feel about the new, no-secrets Abbie?

"We won't know if we don't confront him." She smiled at Baby, who reached intently for the fringes of her scarf. "He's coming over tonight, you know. A date. I say enough with the classroom intellectualizing. Let's get out in the real world and seize a few moments!"

Baby flailed his arms and legs as if that was exactly what he had in mind.

For the second time in a week, Ben stood on Abbie's steps bearing a gift. Chinese food, this time. And this time he didn't try to fool himself into thinking tonight wasn't a date. It was. She'd said it. He'd agreed to it. The start of something new. *What*, he couldn't tell precisely, but he'd decided to follow this road to its conclusion.

Abbie had been that much on his mind the past three days.

She opened the door with an expression that told him she, too, saw tonight as different. "Come in! I hope you brought enough for an army. I'm starved."

He stepped over the threshold, starved as well, but in ways Chinese food wouldn't touch.

"I missed you," he said without preamble. He'd promised himself that this evening he wouldn't beat around the bush.

"I missed you, too." She colored prettily. Something she'd been doing a lot lately. "And worried when I didn't hear from you. Not that you were under any obligation," she rushed on, "but it highlighted in just a tiny way how you must have felt when I disappeared. I'm so very sorry, Ben. If I could turn back time…"

It appeared she, too, had decided not to beat around the bush.

"You told me Tuesday morning at the pier we needed to start fresh." He held out his free right hand, when he would rather have taken her in his arms. "Pax?" It was a ritual they'd used as teenagers, after a quarrel. Something old to go with the new.

"Pax." She slipped her hand in his, her touch warm and soft and smooth. Inviting.

"Where's the bruiser?"

She inhaled as if they'd cleared a major hurdle. "In the kitchen. Thank goodness he stays where you put him. Pat Spenser says to enjoy this stage because he'll be on the move in a few months."

"Enjoy this stage because, as a foster mom, you might not see the next." He felt the need to warn her.

"Ah, yes." She ushered him into the kitchen. "That's something I need to discuss with you. Letting go when the time comes."

"You're asking the wrong person." Hell, he'd flunked letting go on more than one occasion. Setting the take-out containers on the table, then picking Baby up from his car seat, Ben reveled in the clean infant scent, tried to keep the conversation on this bouncing baby boy. On foster care. Where Abbie had intended it. Not on their past failed romantic relationship. "It's hard not to get attached. You can only hope the child has gone to a more stable environment."

"Once he leaves, will we ever see him again?" Her face looked as if it might crumple.

"Sorry, Abbie. That's unlikely."

She'd set two dinner places alongside Baby's car seat. Pensively, she ran her finger around the rim of one plate. "I've tried so hard to stay in the present.

To focus on the moment. I came home to Point Narrows to achieve a balance between acceptance and expectation. But every day since my return, I've been pulled into the past. Into the future.'' She paused as her eyes misted.

''Abbie...'' He returned Baby to his car seat. ''I don't have the answers for me, let alone for you.'' He lifted the take-out containers. ''But I have Hunan chicken and Kung Po shrimp and the night off. And Baby's with us *right now.*''

She quickly traded unshed tears for a smile. ''*Right now* is one terrific place to start.''

Squaring her shoulders, she brought a pot of steeped tea to the table. He opened the take-out containers. Baby found his thumb and sucked on it noisily. Outside, the northeast wind increased, each thrust against the little cottage making the warm kitchen seem more and more like safe harbor. Like home after a long journey. If Ben were honest with himself, he'd rather be here than anywhere else.

''Did your father and brothers survive my outburst at the pier?'' Abbie asked, seating herself across the table from Ben.

''Sure.'' He grinned. ''None of them expected you'd stand up to them. In public, no less. My brothers admire guts, whether they admit it or not. And my father...my father and I had a surprising conversation as a result.''

''How so?''

''Did you know he carries a picture of my mother?''

''I did.'' Two bright patches of pink appeared on Abbie's cheeks. ''He asked me not to tell.''

"Not even me?" He bristled with the sense he'd been left out. Again.

"Especially not you." Abbie took a deep breath and slid her hand across his wrist. "He said you worried enough about your brothers and sister. You didn't need to worry about him."

"I worried anyway."

"Perhaps he thought you wouldn't forgive him for letting go his anger."

Ben clenched his jaw at how she'd hit the mark.

"Why do you suppose he chose to tell you?"

"*My* anger." Although self-disclosure wasn't his favorite pastime, he'd sworn to himself he'd be open and honest. With self-control, the admissions needn't get sloppy. "At the pier you said you didn't want an angry man in your life. Pop told me you were right to feel that way. Told me to let go any resentment I still held on to."

"And?"

He moved his hand out from under hers. Pretended he wanted rice. "You've got to understand my temperament is suited to my line of work. A cop has to foster an edge. A healthy cynicism. Day in and day out we see society's worst side. You've got to get angry to stoke a yen for justice. A forgive-and-forget attitude can get you killed."

"That's a pretty heavy load to carry over into your off-hours." She cocked her head as if challenging him. "I'm a librarian, sure, but I draw the line at cataloging my family recipes by Dewey decimal."

"Yeah, well, for the past eight years I've pretty much been a cop seven days a week, twenty-four hours a day."

"We'll have to see what we can do about that." Her eyes flashed mischief. He could almost believe she flirted with him.

But then she changed the subject. To the weather and the threat of storm. To her parents' scheduled arrival tomorrow. To Baby's growing store of "tricks." To Mariah and her love of reading. To Garrett and the difficulties of single parenthood. To small-town gossip and meddling.

On the surface the meal passed as if they were longtime friends. Or a comfortable married couple. They washed dishes together in Lily Arrondise's old-fashioned kitchen. And put Baby to bed under the low-sloping eaves. All the while they tiptoed over and around the sexual undercurrent that ran undeniably between them.

When they returned to the kitchen, Ben felt as if he'd explode if he didn't touch her. Hold her. Kiss her.

She touched him first.

He'd rolled up his sleeves to give Baby his bath. When he began to roll them down now, she stayed his hand. Ran her fingers over the faded scars on his forearm.

"How did this happen?" There was more than curiosity in her voice. There was heartfelt concern.

"Line of duty. A kid went nuts on drugs. He had a knife. I was lucky he didn't have a gun."

"This happened here? Unbelievable."

"Police work—even small-town police work—comes with no guarantees."

"Because your job's in quiet little Point Narrows, I never stopped to think of the reality. Of the danger."

"I don't focus on the danger." He took her hands in his own. Stood before her and looked directly into her soft green eyes. "I focus on the satisfaction of waking up every morning to work that's useful in a town that respects me. I try to face the task at hand and find fulfillment in each day as it comes."

With his declaration, tears formed on Abbie's lacy lashes. "I know exactly how it feels to seek that focus. But I'm not sure I'm as strong as you."

At the sight of her tears and at the sound of longing in her voice, his self-control slipped irrevocably. He gathered her into his arms.

"Abbie, love, you are one of the strongest individuals I know." He kissed the top of her head, relished the tickle of her fine auburn hair. "You fought the big C and still had energy left over to take on the Chase boys."

When she pulled back to look at him, he saw desire in her eyes. Desire that turned the cool green to molten pools. A desire that mirrored his own.

"I want you," he uttered, his voice ragged, his senses raw.

She stiffened in his arms. "I want you, too, but—"

"There are no *buts* tonight."

"There's reality." Placing her palms flat on his chest, she pushed away. No tears glittered in her eyes. Only an unvarnished truth. And a steely determination. How could she say she wasn't strong? "I'm a woman whose left breast has been cut away."

Could he handle that fact? He gazed into the depths of her eyes, into her very soul. He had loved her physical beauty, yes, but it had been her spirit that had captured his heart. Long ago they'd found a connection that couldn't be confined or defined by the physical. A connection that had never been fully severed.

A connection that made it impossible for him to live life as a whole man without her.

"Left breast, you say?" Trying to control the catch in his voice, he brushed her cheek with the backs of his fingers. "Now I can be closer to your heart."

Abbie caught her breath in a moment of profound realization. She would be safe with this man. This man whom she loved. Had never stopped loving. Before she could reconsider, she slipped her hand around his neck and pulled him into a kiss.

With a groan he bent to angle his mouth on hers, the fit awesomely perfect. They were two halves to a whole. Yin and yang. Why had it taken them so long to rediscover that undeniable fact?

She closed her eyes so tightly she saw stars, threaded her fingers through his thick hair and luxuriated in the feel of him against her body. His arms claimed her. His kiss, hot and demanding, scorched her senses, leaving her feeling purified and renewed. She had been a fool to think she could forget Ben as a lover. He was in her bloodstream. He was a part of her. Running from him had diminished her. She now would reclaim him and in the process make herself whole again.

"Abbie," he murmured, trailing kisses from her mouth, across her cheek, over her eyelids, to her ear. Desire and need reverberated in his heavy breathing.

She ran her fingers over his freshly shaven jaw, down to his square chin, to the cleft that made him appear so rugged. With the pad of her thumb she touched the throbbing of his pulse in his neck and thrilled to the miracle of life straining to burst its boundaries. Thrilled to the miracle of the moment.

"Come," she invited, her voice husky and unfamiliar to her ears. "Upstairs."

"But Baby—"

"Is in the little back bedroom." She splayed her fingers across his chest, drew strength from the hard, heated muscles beneath the surface of his shirt. "I made up the front bedroom for my parents." She cocked her head in mischievous seduction. "Etiquette mavens say you must never put company in a room before you've checked it for comfort."

"I'm beyond the comfort stage, woman," he groaned, pulling her hard against him. His eyes, heavy lidded, simmered with unspent passion. "I could take you here."

Hunger rose in her, a hunger she'd suppressed for too many years for fear of being denied a place at the table. "I dare you."

"Too quick. Too easy." He ran the tip of his tongue over his generous mouth, devoured her with a torrid, lingering regard. "I've waited eight long years for this. I want the works. A soft bed. A panoramic view." He trailed his fingers down her cheek, along her neck, over her shoulder. "I want to see every bit of that beautiful body."

She flinched and looked away, because she suddenly couldn't bear his gaze on her. He might no longer find her body beautiful.

"Abbie, look at me." Without hesitation he grasped her chin in his strong fingers, turned her face so that she had to look him in the eyes. "You *are* beautiful."

"I'm changed." Tears stung the edges of her eyes.

"Aren't we all? What if the shoe were on the other foot?" With his work-hardened hands he caressed her skin, with the pads of his thumbs erased the tears that had spilled to her cheeks. "If I were to lose an arm or a leg in the line of duty, how would you feel about me?"

"A breast is such a sexual icon."

"The loss of an arm or a leg certainly would affect my sexual performance."

She swallowed hard.

"Abbie, this is not about our body parts. This is about *us*." He kissed the corner of her eye where another tear had slipped its boundary. "Answer the question. How would you feel about me if I'd lost an arm or leg?"

"It wouldn't change the way I feel about you, but—"

"But nothing." Lightly he covered her mouth with his and murmured against her lips, "I want to make love to you. Need to make love to you. Don't you feel the same want? The same need?"

She did.

Before he could disappear as in a dream, she threaded her fingers with his and led him by the hand through the house they'd envisioned sharing. Forever. This time around he'd made no promises of forever. He'd promised only to make love to her. Now.

Now was enough.

He followed her up the front stairs, along the upper hallway lit by a single baseboard night-light, into the big front bedroom furnished with an enormous four-poster made up with wedding-white linens. The soft light from the hall filtered into the room, creating a semidark sanctuary. In counterpoint, the wind howled outside.

Her heart pounding, Abbie stopped next to the bed and turned to Ben.

He pulled her to him in a crushing kiss. Full of yearning. And of possession. He ran his hands down her sides, under her sweater. His touch on her bare skin made her burn with long-denied pleasure. Oh, how she had craved touch. Ben's touch.

Hungrily, hastily, she undid his shirt buttons. Slid her hand under the fabric, along the hot planes of his chest. Made him moan.

He pulled away from her. Lifted her sweater over her head. Threw it across the room. Pulled her to him again so quickly she barely felt separated from his body. From his heat. From his raw sexual energy. He nuzzled her neck, nibbled her ear as he undid the clasp of her bra. With a single deft movement, he slid the garment from her shoulders. Let it drop. Stood back to look at her naked from the waist up.

She inhaled sharply as the air slid over her revealed flesh. Revealed, she felt vulnerable. Yet even her vulnerability couldn't quell her desire. Tempering that desire was a dread his passion would disappear at the sight of her scar.

Her badge of courage now made her fearful.

"Abbie," he breathed, placing the flat of his large hand on her chest, along the length of her scar. Like a benediction. "I thank God you didn't die."

There was no revulsion in his voice. No pity. Only

a profound thankfulness quickly replaced by a primal hunger. "I missed you," he growled, pulling her to the bed.

The dam of desire burst. Too long had she denied her sensuality. Too long had she denied herself the wanting of this man. She was like a woman starved. As he skimmed her slacks and panties over her hips, she tugged at the buckle of his belt, freed him from his clothing. Pulled him between the sheets. Between her legs.

She would seize this storm-isolated night without thinking of the future.

"Wait," he growled, reaching not for her, but for his pants on the floor next to the bed. "I have protection."

"Why, Ben Chase, you mean to tell me you planned this?" she teased, flattered and relieved that he, at least, had kept his head.

He loomed above her. "I've been planning this, against my better judgment, since the day you came back to town."

She pulled him into a kiss, pulled him into her senses, into her life. Again. At last.

He entered her. Filled her. Repaired the torn circle of their destiny and healed her womanhood.

"I love you," she whispered at the moment her body gave in to the splintering of passion. She loved him because she now truly loved herself.

Chapter Thirteen

"Temperature's a hundred and four."

The lights hurt her eyes. The siren hurt her ears. The needle in her arm hurt. Hurt. Hurt. The strange faces hovering over her moved their mouths, but she couldn't make sense of their words. She spoke a different language. She slipped and slid away from them on a river hot, fast and powerful. Lava. She was lava. Sensing her phenomenal power, she laughed aloud. Or maybe she dreamed the laugh. Or swallowed the laugh. The laugh was inside her. Hot and racing through her bloodstream.

"Pneumonia, most likely."

Was that her name? No, she was lava.

Long, long ago, the study of volcanoes fascinated her. Now she *was* the volcano. She was the molten river to the sea. She was a fierce energy. Hot. So very hot. And all-consuming.

She was liquid fire. The talking heads floating above her should beware. Get out of her way. She would engulf them. Destroy them. She was a raging force.

Yet it hurt to be a raging force. This rocking descent to the sea was as painful for the lava as for everything in its path.

More lights, a blur of lights, pricked her, tried to catch her, but failed. She was too quick. *Run, run, run as fast as you can. You can't catch me. I'm the lava. Wham! Bam!* She burned and abandoned all that stood in her way.

New sounds tried to catch her. More voices. Too many voices.

"On the count of three, let's move her. All together!" a voice from above demanded. God? "You the parents?"

Parents. The lava wept. She had no parents. She had torched her parents in her quest for the sea.

Yet the one word snagged her, had the power to slow her.

"No. We've called her parents. They're on the way."

They would not get here before the lava hit the sea.

"Get them out of here."

"No! Promise me she's going to be all right!" A young, high voice full of fear. The handmaiden to the volcano? The sacrificial virgin? "We didn't know she'd get this sick."

She wasn't sick. She was the lava.

"Come with me. Let the doctors do their work."

Witch doctors. Laughing at their ineptitude, the lava hurtled toward the sea. Felt the spray. Slowed at last as she slipped under the cool, cool waves.

Firmly holding Baby with one arm, Ben balanced the breakfast tray on the other. He paused in the doorway to the large front bedroom and watched Abbie sleep. Her auburn hair spread out across the pillows, she looked like an angel floating through the clouds. Inexpressibly beautiful, she'd been his for this night.

Her fears concerning her mastectomy and her sexuality had been unwarranted. She was gorgeous. Always had been. Always would be. Neither the years nor surgery could take away her spirit, her vitality, her way of giving herself with sensual abandon. Last night she had given and she had taken as if there were no tomorrow.

She'd even whispered that she loved him, and he'd wanted to tell her how he loved her. But something deep inside had held him back. Silenced the words. Perhaps his reluctance could be explained away by the mere fact that he was not an expressive man. Perhaps. More likely it was the fear that if she'd left him once, she could leave him again.

Sound asleep and cuddled next to him after their lovemaking, Abbie hadn't heard Baby cry out for his three-o'clock feeding. As much as Ben hated leaving their warm bed, leaving her embrace, he'd felt honored to give her the gift of sleep, felt honored to tend to Baby.

Baby of the powerful lungs and the love of pre-dawn companionship. For several hours Ben and the little boy had made the kitchen their fortress as the

wind had battered the sides of the house and the snow
had piled up in drifts, cutting them off from the world.
Ben had suppressed the wish that when reality rode
in with the dawn, Abbie, Baby and he could remain
a threesome. He'd reminded himself to live in the
moment.

At the moment, at six-thirty, they were a family.

And he was as ravenous as Baby had been at three.
He'd scrambled eggs, had made toast. And now he
carried breakfast to Abbie, the woman who'd reawakened his hunger.

"Hey, sleepyhead!" he called out. "Up and at
'em!"

She slithered farther under the covers. Muttered
something about the fact that it was still dark.

"Baby says the middle of the night's the best time
to eat."

"Baby!" Clutching the covers to her, she sat bolt
upright in bed. "Did I miss a feeding?"

"Don't worry. I didn't," Ben reassured her with a
grin. She looked so befuddled, so adorably dishev-
eled, he had to chuckle. "One feeding down. Two to
go." He set the breakfast tray on the nightstand, then
propped Baby on a pillow in the middle of the bed
next to Abbie. "I hope you don't mind a chaperon.
He shows no signs of sleep."

"Around seven he'll go down for his morning
nap."

"Let's make a date for seven, then." Shucking his
clothes, Ben slid under the covers. "Right here. Just
the two of us. I'll count the minutes." He waggled
his eyebrows suggestively.

Abbie feigned shock. "Why, Ben Chase, don't you have a job?"

"Not until I get paged or the snowplow goes by." He placed the breakfast tray between them. "We must have gotten an additional foot of the heavy wet stuff overnight, and there's no letup in sight. It's amazing how crime drops with ugly weather."

Blushing, Abbie pulled the covers up around her neck and nestled back against the pillowed headboard. "I don't find this weather ugly. Do you, Baby?" She tickled the little guy's chin.

"Oh, look, Ben! A smile! Baby's first smile!"

"Gas," Ben retorted, although he had to agree that fleeting gummy grin had looked genuine, had to admit it warmed his heart.

"It was real," she insisted, snapping up a piece of toast. "He's happy. And so am I." She nibbled on the crust in a most provocative manner.

So was Ben. Happy. He loved her. Then why couldn't he tell her?

"Thank you," she said, slipping her hand under the covers, over his thigh. Her smile tugged at that vulnerable spot deep within him even as her touch reignited his thinly controlled desire. "For last night."

"It was mutual," he assured her, grasping her hand, lifting her fingers to his lips.

"No. I had more baggage. You made me leave it at the station. Made me feel like a woman again."

"Ah, Abbie. Illness or disability or time can't erase the fact that you're a woman and I'm a man. That's what it really comes down to. No matter our strengths or our weaknesses, take our clothes off and we're human. No more. No less.''

"This morning I feel superhuman," she breathed, her voice husky. Slipping her hand from his, she nudged a fork in his direction. "Eat your eggs." She winked. "You need to keep up your strength."

Feeling the stirrings of renewed passion, Ben glanced at Baby. "When did you say this child sleeps again?"

"Oh, it won't be long." Her eyes sparkled. "Delayed gratification builds character."

"Hypocrite! What's all this talk of living in the moment?"

She was about to answer him when his pager went off.

"Talk about timing," he groaned. "Is your cell phone handy?"

"It's probably in the kitchen. If you remember, we brought only the essentials to bed with us last night."

Definitely the essentials. Man. Woman. And burning desire.

"I'll be right back." Dreams of renewed passions fading with this page, he slid out of bed. "Hopefully, they only want to know where the copier toner is."

"Baby and I will keep the bed warm."

"You keep the bed warm. Sing the bruiser a lullaby. I think he's feeling very sleepy."

"We can hope." She lay back on the pillows in sensual invitation.

He threw on his shirt. Pulled on his pants. Barefoot, he padded downstairs to look for the phone. He found it on the kitchen counter and punched in the station's number, identified himself to Harold, the clerk on duty.

"Where are you, Chief?"

"One-forty Leeward Road."

"We'll send the plow. You're needed at Southern Medical. They found the baby's mother."

Abbie had spent the day waiting for Ben while snow continued to fall. She'd listened to the list of cancellations on the radio. The town manager had declared all nonessential government offices, including the library, closed.

Abbie's parents had called to tell her their flight that afternoon had been canceled. They would monitor the weather before making alternative reservations. Perhaps they'd aim for the New Year. As much as she'd looked forward to seeing her parents, Abbie relished spending a snowbound Christmas with Ben. She had to stop herself from thinking *with Ben and Baby*.

Baby's mother had been found.

Ben had said he'd get in touch with Abbie as soon as he could tell her the whole story. Morning had gone by, then half of the afternoon, and still no word. Anticipation made her edgy on a day when she should have been basking in the afterglow of making love with Ben. When Baby slept, she tried to sleep, but found herself pacing the cottage instead, rethinking in fragments the events of last night.

Because of Ben's exquisite sensitivity, because of his thorough lovemaking, she'd slept till dawn, missing Baby's 3:00 a.m. feeding. In eight years she hadn't given herself up so completely to sleep. A certain wariness had made her sleep patterns fitful. But last night, in Ben's protective embrace, she'd let go any residual fears.

She had only one regret. In the heat of passion she'd told Ben she loved him. He hadn't responded. Perhaps she'd only imagined saying it. Perhaps he hadn't heard. She hoped as much. She didn't want to make him feel as if this physical reconciliation must force him to commitment. She shouldn't be looking for commitment. Commitment involved the future, while she'd made a vow to live in the moment. She tried not to dwell on last night when a door had opened, letting in a tiny sliver of light from that illusive future.

At two-thirty in the afternoon, as Baby took his afternoon nap, Abbie heard someone stamping his or her feet on the outside steps. *Oh, please, let it be Ben.* She flew to the door, then flung it open in homecoming.

Ben stood before her, fatigue rimming eyes flinty and cold. The set of his shoulders told her he'd changed from the generous lover of last night to a lawman of hard purpose. Yearning to thaw that severe expression, Abbie grasped his hand in both hers and drew him into the warmth of the cottage, back into her sphere of influence.

"I've been in an agony, not knowing!" she exclaimed, pulling him out of his jacket, feeling the cold emanate off him in waves. "What can you tell me?"

"She's just a child herself. Seventeen. Heather Norton. A runaway from Nashua, New Hampshire." He rubbed his arms as if he couldn't get warm.

"You must be chilled through." Abbie drew him

toward the kitchen, felt the resistance in his body.
Sensed an emotional distance between them even as
she held his hand. "Let me fix you tea and a sandwich. You can tell me everything while you eat."

As she prepared the food, he sat in silence at the
kitchen table, his expression tense and faraway as if
he were worrying a thorny matter. Sensing he needed
space and a little time to tell his story, she didn't
question him further, although the waiting had her
stomach churning.

She placed tea and sandwich in front of him, then
sat across from him with a cup of tea for herself. She
could wait no longer. "Start at the beginning," she
urged.

"She was a high school honors student, heading
into her senior year. Slight to start with, she hid most
of the pregnancy with baggy clothing. Hid it from her
parents. A friend of a friend of a friend was a midwife
in a commune in rural Maine. Just before school
started in September, Heather ran away from home,
lied about her age, joined the commune and had her
baby there. October twenty-fifth. He's two months
old."

"Baby?" Abbie felt a tightening in her throat.

Ben nodded. "Justin."

Abbie took a deep breath. She'd always called him
Baby because she knew he had an identity of which
she had no part, of which she could claim no further
connection once his mother returned. Yet when Ben
gave him a name, she felt as if Baby had been
wrenched from her arms.

"Justin," she repeated softly, almost in farewell.

"The members of the commune were a pretty nonjudgmental bunch, but they urged Heather to call her parents. To reconcile. When she thought they might blow her in, she fled again. This time to Portland where she knew a couple kids she'd met in summer camp years ago. One of the kid's parents has a beach house in Point Narrows. Heather used it as a hide-out.''

Abbie inhaled sharply. ''She was here all along?''

''Yeah.'' The muscles along his jaw twitched. ''Right under our noses. Until she came down with pneumonia and dumped Ba...Justin on the library doorstep.''

''She was sick. She knew she couldn't take care of him. She tried to get him help.''

''That's what she claims.'' He narrowed his eyes. ''I think she's just an irresponsible brat brought up in a throwaway society. Otherwise, why wouldn't she do the right thing and call her folks?''

''Maybe her home life was intolerable.''

''Not to meet the parents.''

''They're here?''

''Came as soon as they were called. They're over-come with relief that their daughter's alive. Their life has been on hold these past few months in their panic to find her. They knew how these stories can end.''

''How did they take the news of their grandson?''

''Shock hit them first. Then disbelief that their own daughter wouldn't come to them for help.''

''Why do you suppose she didn't seek their help?''

''The girl, by her own admission, pushed herself to excel. Saw herself as an academic superstar. She was on the fast track to an Ivy League college until the baby derailed her. In her mind, she'd failed so miserably who could possibly love her?" Grim faced, Ben pushed the half-eaten sandwich away from him. "She was self-absorbed to the max."

"Perhaps her parents pushed—"

"I don't think you can lay this one at the feet of the parents. They want their daughter back as soon as she's released from the hospital. They want to help raise Justin while Heather completes her schooling. These are people with heart." He scowled. "Too bad their daughter dumped on them the way she dumped on her own son."

An alarm went off in Abbie's mind. She didn't like the edge in Ben's voice. "Reuniting the three generations sounds like a win-win situation," she replied. "How will Social Services handle it?"

"There will be a hearing."

"And what will happen to Justin until then?"

His expression softened marginally. "Janis will call you. She's going to ask if you'll keep him until his fate's been decided."

"Absolutely."

He threaded his fingers through hers. "You've been good for him."

"He's been good for me." She blinked back tears. "What do you think will happen at the hearing?"

"If the Nortons check out, if they're really as supportive as they appear, if they can provide a good home environment, I think Justin will be returned to his family." He increased the grip on her hands. "Unless I charge Heather with child abandonment."

Abbie felt as if the floor dropped out from under her. "Charge Heather? You said yourself she's but a child."

"She had a kid. She ran away from home and put her family through hell. She dumped her kid—in the middle of winter—on a library doorstep. She's choice impaired, to say the least. Do you want this individual taking care of Justin?"

"But the Nortons—"

"Will have trouble enough raising their daughter." He released her hands, scraped back his chair.

Was this her loving Ben sitting in such stony judgment?

"Have you talked to Heather? Does she want to keep her baby?"

"I think she's lost the right to what she wants. It's all about what's right for Justin."

"My God, Ben, it's too early to decide. Heather's in the hospital with pneumonia. Although her parents must still be in shock, they've expressed a desire to reunite. There's time to see how everyone feels tomorrow and the day after that. I'm more than willing to care for Justin until his mother's fit again."

"I don't think any length of stay in the hospital will make Heather Norton a *fit* mother." He stood, nearly tipping over the chair. "I firmly believe the boy should be placed in foster care and the mother should be prosecuted."

"Ben!" She could see him closing down emotionally. "I thought I knew you. Thought I could count on warmth and empathy beneath that tough exterior. Last night—"

"Last night had nothing to do with Justin."

Her heart breaking, she, too, stood. "It seems it had nothing to do with us, either."

A wail from upstairs made it clear Justin was awake.

"Please, stay," she urged. "I'll bring him down, then we can discuss this further."

"There's nothing to discuss. It's a legal matter. Out of your league."

She felt as if he'd slapped her. "It's a human matter, Ben Chase. If you can't see that, perhaps you'd better turn in your badge."

Without a word, he left. By his dark look and the stiff set of his body and the slam of the front door, she expected he wouldn't return.

Now what?

She could let him go. She could return to her original goal when she'd come home to Point Narrows, of focusing on herself, of creating a sense of balance and quiet hope. The trouble was Ben had rocked any attempt at balance. He'd introduced passionate yearning in quiet hope's place. She'd begun to dream again of marrying him, but she couldn't marry a man who hung on to his anger like a badge of honor.

And then there were the Nortons. Justin and Heather and her parents might not know it, but they needed Abbie to champion them.

Perhaps balance was overrated. What good was a second chance at life if she didn't *live?* Sometimes living meant inching out on that limb. Having come this far, she would not falter. The fruit was in sight.

She picked up the phone and dialed the police station.

Chapter Fourteen

Angry that she'd tried to tell him how to do his job, Ben had ignored the first three messages Abbie had left him. He needed to cool off. The process had taken most of the afternoon.

The patrol-car radio crackled again at seven that evening and Suki's voice broke into his thoughts. "Chief, she says it's an emergency." Suki couldn't be blamed this time for her lack of protocol. There was no code on earth that could cover Abbie Latham. Nevertheless, he understood the message.

"I'll check it out," he replied, doubting any such emergency existed. But what if there was trouble with little Justin? He'd never forgive himself if he didn't respond.

"And, Chief?" Suki added. "For what it's worth,

I don't think you should let Abbie get away. She's exactly what you need.''

Snapping the radio off, he reminded himself to get into a career like Garrett's. Lobsters didn't try to run your life.

On emotional autopilot, he drove down the Leeward Road, turned into Abbie's drive, saw that she'd left a light on for him and wondered if she was ready to see reason. Justin deserved a mother who wouldn't desert him.

Abbie opened the door for him before he reached the top step. ''Thank goodness you've come.''

''What's the emergency?'' He stepped into the foyer, resisting the urge to sweep her into his arms and kiss the two of them back into harmony. Was this any way for a cop to make a call?

''We need to talk.''

She pulled him not into the kitchen, but into the parlor where the Christmas tree twinkled with its lights and ornaments. Where Lily Arrondise's treasures made the room seem like an enchanted wonderland. Where Abbie sat down on an impossibly curlicued chair, like some angel perched on the edge of heaven. She wasn't playing fair. She was aiming for emotional territory he didn't want to explore.

He remained standing. ''Is Justin okay?''

''Oh, he's fine. In bed for the night.''

''What, then?'' He tried not to think that he and Abbie should be in bed for the night.

''I know why you're coming down so hard on Heather Norton.''

''She needs to face the consequences of her actions.''

Abbie took a deep breath. Those cool green eyes wouldn't let him move. "You claim you want to punish this young woman for abandoning her baby when, in reality, you want to punish me for abandoning you eight years ago, want to punish your mother for abandoning you as a boy."

"Don't sugarcoat it." Her words cut him off at the knees, rendering him unable to leave when he most needed to retreat with his professionalism intact. With the chink in his emotional armor still only a pinhole.

"Your mother, Heather and I all had our reasons, no matter how flawed. I can't speak for the others, but I know I regret my decision. By way of apology, I'll be your sounding board. Tell me what you're feeling about all three of us. Give it your best shot. Don't hold back."

"You want me to yell at you? What is this? High-stakes truth or dare?"

She set her chin bravely. "I want you to release the anger and frustration that has you tied up in knots, before it diminishes you. I'll listen."

"I don't need a shrink."

"No, you don't. You need a friend and a lover and a wife. You need me, Ben Chase. But we're never going to make it if you destroy yourself with this punitive attitude." She rubbed her arms as if the room had gone cold. "We're both wounded people. Last night you helped me begin to heal. Tonight it's my turn to help you."

"You don't want to hear what I might say."

"I've survived worse. But you're not going to survive holding the pain inside."

He was sick and tired of holding it inside.

"It hurts, dammit!" The words exploded from deep within. "To be the one left behind. To be the one with no answers. You feel useless. And used." He paced the floor. "I couldn't bring my mother back for Pop or the other kids. I couldn't bring you back for myself. I wasn't even the one to find Heather Norton for Justin."

"Stop keeping score."

He stared at Abbie, amazed at her unflinching attitude.

"The point is Justin's mother has been found," she continued. "When she recovers, she can provide answers to the people she's hurt. Her parents. Not you."

"Not Baby?" He ached inside for Baby.

"Baby won't even remember we fostered him. Your job is to make sure he doesn't remember, to work with Janis to guarantee Heather and the Nortons can deliver on their promise of a loving and stable home."

"Why'd she run in the first place?" An old hurt clawing at his heart, he ran his hand over his chest. "What is it with you women running from the ones who care the most for you?"

Abbie sat very still on the edge of her chair. She barely spoke above a whisper. "*I* came back. To you. To explain."

"But *she* didn't." He ground out the words. He meant his mother.

"No, she didn't," Abbie replied, understanding without question. "And that's a cold, hard fact you have to accept and incorporate into who you are without letting it destroy you. Then you can move on."

Her eyes glistening, she took a deep breath. "Tell me about her leaving."

"No!" He was willing to go only so far. Even when Abbie and he were dating, he'd never told her the specifics of that morning.

"Let it out and let it go."

Hadn't he told Jenni in Portsmouth that holding on against all reason would drag you down, would make you feel so low you wouldn't recognize yourself?

Maybe he ought to listen to the advice he doled out.

Too long he'd covered up his own wants and needs in the name of survival. With her words just now, Abbie had lit a fuse. The emotional powder keg that was his past blew up, shocking him with the high-voltage feelings that coursed through him. He'd always felt as if the telling would kill him. Now he felt as if keeping silent would prove his undoing.

"I came downstairs to eat breakfast before heading out to school," he began, wincing at the memory. "I couldn't smell coffee or bacon frying or bread toasting. It's funny how you can smell the lack of something. The house was dead quiet, too. Creepy. Most mornings the younger kids were making a racket before I even got up. That morning Margot, Sully and Garrett were standing around Pop seated at the table. He had one hand around a whiskey bottle and the other around a balled-up piece of paper. His eyes were flat. Unseeing. The kids looked as if none of them knew what to do."

Ben's skin began to crawl. Abbie didn't move from her seat.

"I walked up to Pop, tried to get the whiskey out

of his hands, but he held on as if life itself were in that bottle. I had better luck with the paper. He let it drop as soon as I touched it.''

''It was from your mother?''

''Yes.'' He felt perspiration dot his forehead. ''I smoothed it on the kitchen table. Recognized my mother's writing. Just a couple lines. The way she might write an excuse for one of us kids being absent from school. Only, this time she was the one absent.''

Something hotter than anger rose in his throat. Tears. He willed them gone. He hadn't cried as a boy of twelve. He sure as hell wasn't going to cry as a man of thirty.

''What did she write?'' Abbie rose from her seat. Crossed the room. Took his hands in hers. ''You never told me.''

'''You've worn me out. I'm leaving before I hurt myself or you or both of us.''' As etched as those words were in his memory, this was the only time he'd spoken them aloud. He felt something break inside.

Holding tightly to Abbie's hands, he could still hear the baby—Jonas—scream for his breakfast. No one had gotten him up. He'd been mad as hell. Miserable. That morning he'd summed it up for the rest of them.

''Your mother knew her limitations,'' Abbie said softly. ''She hurt you in leaving, but she might have hurt you more had she stayed.''

''Dammit!'' He flung Abbie's hands away from him. The anger and frustration at being abandoned by the two women he loved most erupted. ''I'm so sick of people telling me they've hurt me for my own good.''

He paced the room. ''Perhaps I'm powerless to change the past, but I can redirect Heather Norton's future. I can make her accountable for her actions. I can make her understand her decisions affect more than just herself. You can't shed a child—a loved one—as though they're an unwanted overcoat.''

Pain had his chest in a vise.

Abbie stepped in front of him. '''She abandoned me. She mistreated me. She betrayed me.' Harboring such thoughts keeps anger alive. Acknowledge those thoughts, then release them and release the anger. Anger doesn't dissolve anger. Sometimes even understanding doesn't dissolve it. Only compassion dissolves anger. Let it go, Ben.''

''I can't.''

''Yes, you can. I believe in you. You can choose to have a big heart.''

He stood frozen between a self-protective need and a longing to do the right thing.

She clutched his arms. Shook him soundly. ''Think about how prosecuting Heather will further the chain of abandonment. Her parents, having lost their daughter once, will lose her twice. They will, in addition, lose a grandson they didn't know they had and now look forward to loving. And Justin will lose his mother and a set of grandparents.''

The passion in her voice seemed to emanate down to her fingers. Into his arms. ''But allowed to return to his mother,'' she continued, ''who would return to her parents, who are willing to help forge a new family configuration, Justin might have a head start in the family-love-and-secure-roots department.''

This was coloring outside the lines.

But hadn't he colored outside the lines just recently? With Jenni in Portsmouth? Hadn't giving her a second chance made him feel a better man? And Jenni was only a stranger. Heather Norton was Baby's mother. Baby. Justin. A tiny boy he'd grown to love.

''You hold their fate in your hands,'' Abbie continued. ''If Heather Norton truly wants custody of her baby, if the Nortons truly make an effort to help her provide a stable home, will you accept responsibility for taking Justin away from his mother? Can you put yourself in Justin's place when he's older? Can you, Ben?''

He could. He turned his back on Abbie. The dam of emotion broke. He wept. Great silent tears that wet his cheeks and released the pressure on his heart.

She came up behind him. Thrust her arms under his arms, around his chest. Pressed her face to his back. ''Say it.''

Shuddering, he held it in no longer. ''I miss her.''

Abbie said nothing. She held him from behind while the years flooded over him. He sat again at the family dinners where the Chases had closed ranks around the place that had been his mother's at the table. He replayed the sporting events where she hadn't shared in his victories. He felt the wintry chill of Christmas without a woman's touch. Without a mother's touch.

''I saved that stupid Christmas present,'' he whispered, his throat raw, the tears having run their course.

"The last one she gave you?"

"Yeah. It was a recording of my favorite group at the time."

"Do you still have it?"

"No. I kept it and played it when the others weren't around. When you left, I heaved it into the harbor."

"That was a start," Abbie said against his back. "Now heave the rest of your anger there, as well."

"I missed you, too," he breathed, the words barely audible. "I missed you."

"I'm here." She squeezed him tightly. "I'm home."

The tears hadn't yet cooled on his cheeks when the strangest thing happened. The pain, the frustration and the bitterness slowly seeped out of him. Abbie, with her candor and her constant reaching out, had gained purchase in his granite heart, like a pine seedling taking root on a barren, rockbound island. Only, her seedling bore the germ of forgiveness.

"I can't take Justin away from his mother," he admitted. "Not if she and her parents can provide a real family."

Slowly Abbie turned him around to face her. Wiped the dampness from his cheeks. "And what about me? Can you forgive me?"

He already had, although he hadn't admitted it to himself. He thought of his father, who'd come to a secret forgiveness from which he'd gained no benefit. Because he'd never let anyone close enough to share his burden, Tobias had undergone no real healing.

Ben wanted to heal.

This woman standing before him—this woman who seemed to know him better than he knew himself—had led him through his anger to a cooler place, a place wherein she'd anointed him with the therapeutic balm of compassion. Of love.

"I've forgiven you. I just wasn't man enough to tell you."

"Are you saying you're not perfect?" She cocked her head, and mischief twinkled in her eyes.

"Far from it."

"Good. Perfection makes me nervous." Taking his face in her hands, she stood on tiptoe and planted a kiss full on his mouth as if she were bestowing a prize.

He certainly felt himself a winner.

Abbie backed away from the luscious feel of Ben's warm lips. For a while she'd thought she might lose him. But now she saw the haunted look slowly fade from his eyes. She wasn't naive enough to think they'd effected a cure tonight, but they'd begun the journey to recovery. Together.

"You know," she added, feeling fearless in her ability to share anything with him, "when you forgo perfection, you learn to see possibilities in the most improbable places."

"Such as?" He drew her back into his arms.

"Well…Heather, by her rash behavior, brought you and me face-to-face again where we could confront the pain of the past. Could move beyond it. In an unlikely way, she played a part as our guardian angel."

"So you're telling me guardian angels can put you through hell?" He shook his head, ironic disbelief in his eyes.

"All I'm saying is that anything's possible. This is

the season of miracles, you know.'' She ran her fingers over the sculpted planes of his face, relieved to feel no tension. ''You and I have the power to make our own miracle by allowing ourselves a second chance.''

For an instant she wasn't sure if she'd gotten through to him. But then the residual pain disappeared from his eyes, replaced first by overwhelming relief, and then by a passionate intensity.

''How I love you!'' he murmured, bending his head to kiss her.

''I love you,'' she sighed before his mouth captured hers. It was pure heaven to be able to admit it freely. Slipping her arms around his neck, she gave herself up to the sensation of her body pressed to his. Of their lives melded. Again.

He deepened the kiss. Swept his tongue across her lips. Made her blood race. To think they were together again. With no dark past dividing them. Only clothing between them. And they would soon dispense with that. She felt it in the way his mouth possessed her, in the way his hands claimed her, in the way he strained against her.

While he trailed kisses down her neck, she pulled him closer, whispered in his ear. ''To bed.'' She felt sexy and womanly and just a little bit wanton.

''On one condition.''

''Condition!'' She pulled away, feigning shock. ''You're putting conditions on this relationship already?''

''Absolutely.'' He smiled, a smile that filled his eyes and made his handsome face light up. ''Now, hush.''

"Hush, is it?" She stuck her hands on her hips. "I suppose you'll be wanting me to walk two steps behind you next."

"Oh, no. I let you out of my sight once. I won't do it again."

She liked the idea of staying right where he could see her. "What, then?"

His eyes turned more gray than blue, as soft as fog on a winter's morning. "Abbie Latham, will you marry me?"

She inhaled sharply. Her first response was to warn him that she couldn't promise him forever, but then she remembered her grandmother urging her to go out on a limb for the sweetest fruit. She remembered how Murphy was a reminder to seize the day. She remembered how, with Justin, she had touched the future. Perhaps forever was just a series of moments strung out across a life, a lovely succession, like beads on a string.

She could handle a forever like that.

"Oh, yes!" she exclaimed, throwing her arms around Ben's neck. "I'll marry you, yes!"

"Then to bed!" He clasped her hand and led her to the front hall.

Laughing, they scrambled up the stairs in such a mad rush, Miss Lily's knickknacks rattled on the treads. At the head of the stairs, Ben scooped Abbie into his arms. "Why wait for tradition?" he growled hungrily.

When he tried to carry her through the doorway to the front bedroom, he bumped the door, which swung back against the wall with a tremendous bang.

Down the hall Justin awoke. And complained.

Abbie could feel the soft rumble of Ben's laugh deep in his chest. "He might be the son of an unlikely angel," he remarked, putting her down gently, "but he has the devil's own timing."

"I'll settle him down." Abbie placed a finger on Ben's lips. "Don't go anywhere."

As she turned to leave, singing rose from below. Ben moved to the bedroom window. "Carolers. Bring Justin in here. This is too good to miss."

Abbie hurried down the hall to Baby's room. When she picked him up, he calmed immediately. She kissed his forehead. "You needed reassurance, that's all. That won't change with age," she told him as she returned to Ben.

Standing at the window, Ben held his arm out to her. Holding little Justin, she slipped into his warm embrace. "A rain check on the you-know-what," he murmured huskily against her hair.

"You'd better start spelling," she warned, a smile wreathing her lips and contentment hugging her heart. "I have a feeling Justin's one smart boy."

As the three of them listened to the holiday serenade, Abbie felt at peace in the moment. She'd come home to find herself and had found much, much more. She'd discovered a doorway to the future in Justin and a deep and abiding love in Ben.

Epilogue

"To life!" With unchecked tears in his eyes and a broad smile on his face, Grant Latham turned to his daughter, Abbie, and raised high a goblet filled with sparkling cider in a warm New Year's Day toast.

Up until nine years ago he'd traditionally said, *Long life,* but now his family knew to be satisfied with, knew to revel in, life without the modifiers.

Abbie raised her goblet in turn to each of the people at her table. Her mother, Celeste. Her husband, Ben. Her new friends, Elizabeth and Karl Norton. Their daughter, Heather. And Heather's one-year-old son, Justin. Baby. Abbie and Ben's godson.

"To life!" they chorused. How sweet the sound.

To be alive was a miracle for which Abbie gave thanks daily.

"To Heather!" Elizabeth Norton declared. "Who's

just been named to the governor's honor program in science.''

"To family!'' Karl exclaimed, beaming upon Elizabeth, Heather and Justin. "And to Abbie and Ben, who brought us back together. Safe and sound. I still can't find words to thank you.''

Ben wrapped his free hand around Abbie's, around the gold band on her finger. "To a new year and fresh starts!'' His touch both excited and calmed her. As it always had.

Celeste wiped tears from her eyes. "To every mother's baby. Big and small!''

Heather snuggled a wriggling Justin and looked as if she was trying hard not to cry. "To food, for crying out loud! We're starving!''

Abbie's heart swelled with joy as she watched Ben stand to carve. He was her soul mate after all.

"Starving? Then we'll serve from youngest to oldest this year,'' he said, grinning at Justin. "What'll it be, big guy? Roast beef or tofu-disguised-as-turkey?''

"Tofu-turkey, of course,'' Heather replied with mock horror before her son could answer. "You know we're vegans, Chief.''

Justin caught his mother in an exuberant bear hug.

"With lots of mashed potato to play in,'' Abbie teased as she spooned the fluffy white vegetable on Justin's plate.

"You're giving him his bath, then.'' Heather took the plate for Justin.

"Now, that's a hardship I'll try to bear.'' Abbie shot Justin a wink and laughed aloud when he blinked both eyes in return. "Who taught you that?''

Justin pointed a finger at Ben.

Ben feigned chagrin, and Abbie stood on tiptoe to kiss him on the cheek.

This godson—this child of a child—had been a blessing to the two of them. With Justin, Abbie was more hopeful because she had already touched the future. With Justin, Ben was less angry because he had let go of a piece of the past. Together they had learned that, with love, obstacles can turn into opportunities.

Ben carved and Abbie served up the side dishes until it came time to fill Abbie's plate. Instead of beef or tofu-turkey, Ben placed a pink, folded piece of paper on a plate, then set it in front of her.

"What's this?" Abbie looked into Ben's eyes, eyes filled with love and more. Satisfaction.

"Unfold it."

She did and found a "While you were out…" message from Serena Hopkins. "The Arrondise heirs have accepted your purchase offer on the cottage."

"Oh, Ben!" Abbie flung her arms around Ben's neck. "It's ours! It's finally ours!"

"It's always been ours." He squeezed her tightly to him. "But now we'll have the deed."

In coming home to Point Narrows to find a sense of balance, she'd found renewed passion and an unexpected sense of family.

"I love you," she declared, planting a kiss on the cleft in Ben's chin.

"I love you right back," he replied with a playfulness that scarcely concealed his sensuous nature.

"Le's eat!" Justin declared, hauling them all back into the moment. The present. A precious gift.

* * * * *

▼™ SILHOUETTE®
SPECIAL EDITION™

AVAILABLE FROM 15TH MARCH 2002

AN ABUNDANCE OF BABIES Marie Ferrarella
That's My Baby!

Delivering Stephanie Yarbourough's babies in a car park was a unique way for Sebastian Caine to reintroduce himself to his old flame. And with Stephanie planning to raise the babies alone, he kept dropping by just to help…

THE MILLIONAIRE AND THE MUM
Patricia Kay
The Stockwells

Mercenary Jack Stockwell had a mission to find out if his family had swindled Beth Johnson's ancestors out of a fortune. The strong, earthy woman and her two children stirred feelings deep within him. But how would Beth feel when she discovered that her lover was actually a Stockwell?

A LOVE BEYOND WORDS Sherryl Woods

Vulnerable Allie Matthews preferred her life risk-free—until Ricky Wilder pulled her from the rubble of her home and coaxed her out of her cautious world. Could she trust her life to the sexy fire-fighter who lived his whole life on the edge?

THE MARRIAGE MAKER Christie Ridgway
Montana Brides

Ethan Redford proposed marriage—and motherhood—to Cleo Kincaid Monroe expecting a 'yes'. After all he knew being a bride and a mum to little Jonah was Cleo's dream. But Ethan's honour demanded that he must not take advantage of his virgin bride!

HIDDEN IN A HEARTBEAT Patricia McLinn
A Place Called Home

From the moment Rebecca Dahlgren stepped onto Far Hills Ranch, Luke Chandler was hard to miss, with his sexy broad chest and his sleepy eyes that weren't interested in sleeping. This 'strictly business' consultant knew she was about to get into trouble!

BABY OF CONVENIENCE Diana Whitney

Laura Michaels needed a powerful husband to keep custody of her son—and millionaire Royce Burton needed a wife. So they made a deal: marriage—for the baby's sake.

0302/23a

Fortune's Children
THE GROOMS

Welcome back to the drama and mystery of the Fortune dynasty

Fortune's Children: The Grooms—
five strong, sexy men
surrounded by intrigue, but
destined for love and marriage!

*The Fortune's Children legacy
continues in this popular continuity
series with two new books a month.*

Diana Palmer

THE TEXAS RANGER

He has a passion for justice

Published 15th March 2002

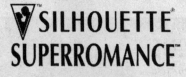

1201/SH/LC27

SILHOUETTE®
INTRIGUE™
is proud to present

TOP SECRET BABIES

These babies need a protector!

Unwrap the mystery

FREE
2 BOOKS
AND A SURPRISE GIFT!

We would like to take this opportunity to thank you for reading this Silhouette® book by offering you the chance to take TWO more specially selected titles from the Special Edition™ series absolutely FREE! We're also making this offer to introduce you to the benefits of the Reader Service™ —

    ★ FREE home delivery   ★ FREE gifts and competitions
    ★ FREE monthly Newsletter   ★ Exclusive Reader Service discount
         ★ Books available before they're in the shops

Accepting these FREE books and gift places you under no obligation to buy; you may cancel at any time, even after receiving your free shipment. Simply complete your details below and return the entire page to the address below. **You don't even need a stamp!**

YES! Please send me 2 free Special Edition books and a surprise gift. I understand that unless you hear from me, I will receive 4 superb new titles every month for just £2.85 each, postage and packing free. I am under no obligation to purchase any books and may cancel my subscription at any time. The free books and gift will be mine to keep in any case.

E2ZEC

Ms/Mrs/Miss/Mr ....Initials..............................
                                                 BLOCK CAPITALS PLEASE
Surname..
Address...

....

....Postcode ....

Send this whole page to:
UK: FREEPOST CN81, Croydon, CR9 3WZ
EIRE: PO Box 4546, Kilcock, County Kildare (stamp required)

Silhouette® is a registered trademark used under licence.
Special Edition™ is being used as a trademark.